P

"Noonan's back catalogue covers a great deal of ground, and pretty much humps the shit out of it."

—David Roth, *VICE*

"I adore Lacey Noonan's writing style."

—Leonard Delaney, *author of Conquered by Clippy*

"Lacey Noonan has truly catapulted herself, however knowingly, into the pantheons of greatest American authors (F. Scott Fitzgerald, Mark Twain, etc.), greatest female American authors (Willa Cather, Toni Morrison, etc.), and greatest humans (Jesus, Julius Caesar, etc.) to have ever set foot on this great Earth we call home."

—Brenden, *amazon reviewer*

"...one of the literary masters of our time..."

—Jonathan C. Pike, *amazon reviewer*

PRAISE FOR *I DON'T CARE IF MY BEST FRIEND'S MOM IS A SASQUATCH, SHE'S HOT AND I'M TAKING A SHOWER WITH HER ...BECAUSE IT'S THE NEW MILLENNIUM*

"It's somewhere between 'Ulysses' and 'iPad for Dummies'. Closer to the latter though."

—herbalt, *amazon reviewer*

"Anyhoodle, [this book is] frigging hilarious... From the copyright pirate warning, to the chapter headings, to line after line of really funny prose, this short is full of whip-sharp dialogue and clever turns of phrase."

—Acesfull, *amazon reviewer*

Praise for *A Gronking to Remember*

"We were made aware this weekend that Gronk erotica exists and is being sold on Amazon. Due journalism diligence insisted we purchase this Gronk erotica, give you a full review, and then turn it into an animated movie."

—*Deadspin*

"'Lacey Noonan,' an author—nay, an American hero—recently penned one of the greatest works of fan fiction we here at Complex Sports had ever seen... We're talking highbrow shit here."

—*Complex*

"It's been a slow year for people who have been looking for NFL-related erotica novels, but the drought is finally over thanks to author Lacey Noonan (Not pictured above)."

—*CBSSports.com*

"Rob Gronkowski might just be the hero that the world of erotica needs right now."

—*Inquisitr.com*

"Rob Gronkowski Erotica Is Here and It's... Something."

—*Boston.com*

"The western canon is scattered with watershed works of literature penned by American authors...add A Gronking to Remember to that list."

—Brenden, *amazon reviewer*

"I don't want to live in a world where this book doesn't exist."

—David B. Hansen, *amazon reviewer*

"Thought this was going to be about the hash browns at Dunkin' Donuts. Disappointing!"

—happykins, *amazon reviewer*

a

The Dishes Are Done Man!

book

BOOKS BY *Lacey Noonan*

NOVELLAS

Seduced by the Dad Bod: Book One in the Chill Dad Summer Heat Series

Hot Boxed: How I Found Love on Amazon

The Babysitter Only Rings Once

I Don't Care If My Best Friend's Mom is a Sasquatch, She's Hot and I'm Taking a Shower With Her . . . Because It's the New Millennium

Eat Fresh: Flo, Jan and Wendy and the Five Dollar Footlong

A Gronking to Remember

A Gronking to Remember 2: Chad Goes Deep in the Neutral Zone

NOVELS

Shipwrecked on the Island of the She-Gods: A South Pacific Trans Sex Adventure

COLLECTIONS

The Hotness: Five Burning Hot Novellas

I Don't Care if My Sasquatch Lover Says the World is Exploding, She's Hot But I Play Bass and There's Nothing Hotter Right Now Than Rap-Rock

(...Because It's the New Millennium • Book 2)

LACEY NOONAN

ISBN: 1519381131
ISBN-13: 978-1519381132

Special Thanks

Salami, Ray Cho, and J.J. Finestone IV,
and to Scary Karl's big foot…

CONTENTS

To Rob Delaney, person of hair

I Don't Care if My Sasquatch Lover Says the World is Exploding, She's Hot But I Play Bass and There's Nothing Hotter Right Now Than Rap-Rock

...Because It's the New Millennium

"So come to the pond,
or the river of your imagination,
or the harbor of your longing,
and put your lips to the world.
And live
your life."

—Mary Oliver

"My lifestyle's wild, I was living like a wild child."

—Crazy Town

CHAPTER ONE
Large Marges in the Flesh and Fur

We rode by night. The stars above us, the wind in our hair. We made love in thickets, behind dumpsters, in suburban pools, stroked ourselves raw in streams filled with industrial runoff. We didn't care. We were in love and on the run. Love—I can say it was love with no compunction, but there was a lot of lust mixed in there too. Animal goddamn lust. The sex dust that gets in your eyes. Maybe it was because we were so new, but I saw no end in sight to our delicious bone-seshes of the universe. No sooner would I unload myself with spine-shivering glee into Starla's giant, hirsute body in some cool, relieving pond than the crotch rocket's vibrations would renew our passions and we'd have to pull off and scamper into the woods again like two teenagers to bask in the glories and grip of our bodies, our moans of ecstasy wiggling up into the galaxies overhead like a mystical prayer. We ate mostly squirrels. And pinecones. Needless to say, our going was slow—wherever it was Starla was taking us—but it didn't matter. It was the best of times, and it was the hella better of times… It was the new millennium.

We rode by night. Two spirits in the holy dark. I clutched my lover Starla like I was a little baby in a papoose on its mother's back, hidden from the motorcycle wind. I let my fingers play through her soft hair, and let her soft, sentient hair play with my fingers, my mind wandering through the aisles of memories of recent delight and ardor as we busted ass through the blackness. The highway uncoiled before us. Miles and miles of it on our journey—our escape from her evil oppressors, the Lemaires—to a sanctuary where we could let our cross-kingdom love bloom unfettered. As our higher minds were dulled with passion and the single purpose of escape, the road ahead became a ghostly gray singularity in the one headlight, like the Wallflowers' mega-hit single "One Headlight." And, oh, how the bike engine whined. It became our love song: a sustained high note of eternal devotion, like a chant at 998 cc's. I urinated, or crapped if I had to, right off the back of the bike. The highway was like a conveyer belt my poop disappeared on. Starla instinctively knew to take back roads, the highways less traveled, so that we wouldn't be seen by curious, ignorant human eyes, but every once in a while we'd come up to an eighteen-wheeler in the wee hours of night and jet by it. I mean just *blow* by the thing. I always turned to look at the drivers though, to see their faces. Half the time they didn't notice us. But sometimes they did. They would shake from their dolorous, dead-eyed stare and look up and see a twelve foot female sasquatch—sexy as fuck, big ol' booty wiggling and jiggling, straddling our rice rocket, and a naked, bare-assed frat boy (me) hanging onto her for dear life like a kite flapping in a hurricane. I waved. Frequently there was also an erection waving. The drivers waved back slowly, eyes wide, jaw a-dangling. And then we were gone. Boom. Zoom. One hundred and ten miles per hour of screaming love disappearing into the truck driver's amphetamine-fueled delusions. Who would believe them anyway? We were freeway phantoms. An *X-Files* episode on two wheels. Large Marges in the flesh and fur. I laughed joyously into Starla's back, as big as a mountain carpeted with shag, her luscious hair whipping in the onslaught, and I snuggled into her warm, warmer, warmest body, her softness flexed against the wind. Life was so wild and amazing.

We rode by night. "My pet, my lover, but where are we going?" I would murmur the question of the century and nibble on her ear. The motorcycle wobbled. Starla giggled. "Ssh! Not now, my babe of the woods!" she shouted into the wind. Her melodious giggle always made me hard and I forgot what the hell I was asking. It was like a feminine magic spell that sent all the blood in my brain to my dick. My erection pressed into her back as I clutched her body. And soon enough her rump, two sweet cheeks as big as bean bag chairs, would start grinding on me with minds of their own like two separate booty dancers in Will Smith's "Will 2k" video from his 1999 album *Willennium*. Starla would peel back on the throttle and the bike slowed to a stop on the side of the road. Down went the kickstand with a click. And then off into the darkness we went, hand-in-paw to scandalize some trees and ferns. After sniffing out a pond or a pool, the woods would come alive with splashing, squishes and hoots. It happened over and over. We were always going and stopping and going and stopping… I never knew where the road was leading. We'd escaped my dumbass friend Luke and his ding-dong family—verily, the whole modern world—into a realm of animal bliss, Eden innocence, campestral copulation—but still we peeled rubber into the night on our steed of steel, only to stop and peel back the skins, no rubber, and do the deed and sign the deal. Fuck if it wasn't the new millennium…

The days? We slept by day. Doy… That's just what you do. Escape is a nocturnal smooth move Ex-Lax; the guiding North Star evaporates with all her sisters into the ocean of bright blue sky above. At the first sign of dawn, Starla pulled the Yamaha *YZF-R1* off the highway. We'd tuck the motorbike into bed under a camouflage of leaves and branches and then curl up next to it and doze off. If I'm being honest, I think I liked the days better. I was naked. Starla was my lover, but she was also my blanket. She would curl up like a mamma bear and I'd fold myself into her, purring, cooing, rubbing our bodies absentmindedly in the twilight of slumber—something semi-chaste that used to be called "heavy petting" in Victorian times—until warmth and sleep overtook us. As the morning sun gooed through the leaves I'd fall asleep happy knowing that in only a few short hours of rest we'd be balling again like rabid rabbits. That was how we spent our days.

Oh, the days… The days, the days. Little did I know that in only nine more of them, Earth would be blown to bits.

Chapter Two
Rendezvous Perdu

Starla fingers the heavens. I follow her hairy digit across the night sky, planted all over with stars like a moist and glowing garden.

"There," she says, and sighs.

Night has fallen, we've had our bushmeat breakfast and are about to hit the road. But first—an astronomy lesson. I jump up on her lap and follow her gaze.

And I look…

It is a star like any other. But between the galactic spray, a star glimmers like the twinkle in my beloved's eye and I know instinctively it is her home. (Or a planet near there, I suppose.)

"What's it like?" I ask.

"Beautiful."

"Nice."

"So much hair."

"Really?"

"So much delectable hair everywhere, you wouldn't believe it. Strands of it for miles. Mountains of hair. Thousands of feet tall. Rivers. Cities. Governments. Whole economic systems and philosophies."

"Nice."

With wide-eyed wonder I admire her star and its

smoky galaxy between the trees above and wonder what it could all mean. Could I *really* leave Earth? Even if you excluded the fact that there was a homicidal family with laser guns after our hides, there seemed no reason to stay, except perhaps for the Jägermeister, which was really good. The memory of my family, my regular-ass family and the family of wild friends I'd cultivated since, did give me a pang of remorse, but it disappeared quickly. Earth was the pits if you thought about it. I'd extinguished all its wildness. There was nothing left—the new millennium had made that very clear. Or in my quest for the ultimate Wild Ride™, I'd discovered Starla: the totally wildest babe in the whole galaxy. The time last Christmas Break when I fingered my cousin's family's au pair, Friedegunde, in a booth at a Carrabba's Italian Grill paled in comparison. That was filed in the Jason Field's Canon under "wild," yeah, but it wasn't "Skipping Earth With My Sasquatch Baby Wild."

As cool-as-hell as everything was, I did have doubts, though.

There was the niggling thought in the back of my head that if I saw Starla off safely on her rescue ship, then that would be enough excitement in the *Wild Department* for a while and the Lemaires would leave me alone after that. Plus: It *was* the new millennium: the new century, the new decade—had I already extinguished all the possibilities, or was there some new stuff I could get into, raw dog, if I only waited it out?

It seemed that I was looking for reasons to stay too. *Could I leave Starla*, my brain asked. *No*, my dick answered, and in this way, my body went back and forth, like two fervent arguments in the *Armageddon* vs. *Deep Impact* debate.

I was ready for it though—come what may. Life is a mystery. Everyone must stand alone. I look at Starla's star and it feels like home.

"How long will it take us to get there?" I ask.

Starla toots out a sad hoot. A melancholy wave ripples on her body hair.

What have I said? I should really try to be encouraging, I think to myself. Positivity: that's what it's all about now in The New Mill. Like, keep it grunge, for sure—but sunny and *positive*. Like a cool retro 7" of "Don't Steal my Sunshine" b/w "Might as Well Be Walking on the Sun."

"Sorry," I say, nestling in. "I'm sorry. What's the matter? Is it *too* far? When is the spaceship coming to pick us up?"

"As to that I do not know, male component. We must get to a selected rendezvous point. There is no way to contact another vessel until we are there."

"Hmm. Your family though…"

"Are consistently at bay, it is true. I do not know where, though I do not detect them with my olfactory system, which is more powerful than your planet's most sensitive canine units. That I do not perceive their location is why we must travel at such high velocity. I wonder at our lovemaking and showering sessions as well."

"What about them?"

"And I am going to be honest with you, Homo Sapien lover. Truth is demanded in any partnership."

"Truth. True. What is it?"

"I do not possess knowledge of the whereabouts or when the rendezvous will take place."

"Err… Nice?"

Chapter Three

Tenderoni-Style on Wisps of Ethereal Sexmagik

The night I join the Rap Rock Pantheon begins like all the others…

We shake the earth fucking like feral ferrets.

Sounds of the forest wake me. It is evening, soft and supple. The sun has fallen through the trees; the moon has risen. A lavender gray light infuses the cool air around us in our clearing and cricketsong insinuates itself into my dreams: *chirrup, chirrup*, now I'm rubbing my legs together too… *chirrup, chirrup*, like a philharmonic of frottage… *chirrup, chirrup*, oh Mother Nature is surely on a sex registry for the instincts she has instilled in all her creatures…

I am awake now but my eyes are still closed. Starla's giant tongue is investigating my face. Always the early riser. I stiffen downstairs. My legs spread on their own. Leaves crunch under my butt.

"Good morning, Starshine," I mumble and reach for her torso. She is everywhere, all around me: a hair house. I stretch and begin to fondle what I can find. Her breasts, her hairy nipples spring to attention. I rub them up and down. Curled up inside her body for hours, her perfume is like an intoxicating fog. Jasmine, skunk, pollen, rose hips, fruit too long on the vine, ancient compost, hot November rain—Starla's pheromones are my wake and bake. "Oooh…" I moan, druggily, sex-horny.

"Pet," she coos.

"Mmm…"

And Starla moans too. My monstrous lover opens her mouth wide and wraps her maw around the edges of my face. I feel the press of her teeth on my skin. Saliva drips all over my forehead, my nose, my chin. It hits my mouth and I slurp some in, sticky and gooey and magical.

I begin to gyrate my hips, slide forward and press my morningwood against her furry stomach. She groans assent. This is exactly what she wanted. Pleasure!

My brain goes dumb. Awake only thirty seconds and I am already reverting back to an animal state of conscious unconsciousness—the call of the wild—barely vertebrate—American primitive. My eyes roll towards the back of my head. I grip her body hair. "Oh my God, that feels so amazing," I say, the poet laureate of sasquatch poonanny.

Then she does it.

Starla sucks my head up into her mouth down to the top of my shoulders. It is my favorite thing, being a part of her like this, a sex-morsel. I moan in my new cave of darkness. Then she hums… bass-heavy vibrations—like a gong, they wobble down my body, dark and deep. It is a sonic massage. Bass is the best. My body shakes and flops on the forest floor. My dick hardens to stone; I shove my hips forward and her hair swirls around my shaft, the strands curl and envelope my balls like an elegant hand—the hand of a begloved, bitchy but louche Countess or maybe Baroness.

"Do you like that, Jay Jason?" Starla says all around

my head. Her voice is like my inner voice.

"Glrrp glgg," I respond to that voice. Incoherent. Though this is my favorite thing, lately a note of unpleasantness has begun to creep into the act.

For the third day in a row now, that big hanging piece of flesh that Tweety Bird pounds on inside Sylvester the Puddy Cat in all those cartoons, like a speed bag at the top of Starla's mouth, leans forward. It presses against my face and it is hard to breathe. Though I am all about pleasure, I have no desire to die this way yet—that auto-erotic asphyxiation move pure pervs always die trying. I pull my head back and inhale air from her perfumed lungs blowing up from her esophagus. My vision sparkles with oxygen intake and it's on again. "Wowee Zowee!" I echo all inside her head.

A tractor trailer whizzes by on the highway and Starla's stomach hair strokes my cock, tender, loving, Tenderoni-style on wisps of ethereal sexmagik.

Heavenly pleasure surges from every part of my body. My body shakes. And in this shaking, my feet fly forward and make contact with her. My feet are just able to reach the sex between her legs. It is soft and wet, squishy between my toes. She is turned on. I begin kneading her special place. I run my tootsies up and down her feminine lips. Starla moans and I continue to work her alien, simian vagina with my twinkling toes. I tap dance through her two lips.

Her stomach hair strokes my dick quickly now, working the shaft, cupping the balls like an egg cup, which is a thing. Starla is a sex master, possibly the greatest this planet has ever seen.

I am about to blow my load. "I'm coming, Starla," I

whisper on throaty and fluted golden wings. "I'm coming so good, I'm cooooooooming…"

"Who is coming?" she replies all around my head.

"Me?"

"No."

"What?"

"No, it is…" Starla suddenly jumps up. My body falls to the leaves, cold, so very cold and dry and very un-cummed on nor juicified. I look up, dazed and bemused, head and eyes gooey like a newborn kitten. She is on high alert. "No, *someone* is coming."

"I know! I was about to come!" I shout.

"Desist communication," Starla shushes me, pinches my lips closed with her hairy index finger and thumb. "Someone *else* is coming," she whispers, her haunches up, her hair bristling for danger…

Chapter Four
Christ in a Crack House

Quickly, I sit up and look around in every direction.

I am scared.

Naked. Quivery. I wipe the goo from my face.

Christ on a crouton, this is *exactly* what I need right now. Just about to nut whole-hog and the Lemaires start blowing the forest apart with their laser fucking rifles and for what? To keep beauty itself locked away in a cage… for what?

But there is nothing save the silent night woods, every which way but loose. About a hundred yards over a slight rise is the highway. The sound of the occasional car or truck reaches us, their headlights angling the shadows of the trees. There is nothing else. I hear nothing else but crickets, my breath and Starla's preparatory growls.

"Where? What is it, Starla?" I whisper. "Your family? Them?"

After another tense couple of minutes, Starla straightens her back and stands up. She is as big as a tree. And much sexier than one. I look up at her body, so rich with acreage after acreage of sexy and shapely lady parts. Her hourglass figure, much like Green Acres, it is the place to be. I would like to hoe that fertile field. I would like to fork that hay. I would like to tote that barge. "No. I *sensed...* something," she says, sniffing the wind, staring into space. "I guess it is nothing. Something was close, but it moved away."

"What was it?"

"I do not know."

"Christ in a crew cut, Starla. You scared me!"

"Apologies, human male lover."

My cock and balls down in the leaves call unto me, pronounce themselves once more eager for coitus. "Ahh fuhgeddaboudit!" I say, and wrap my body around her hairy telephone pole of a leg.

Instantly I am hornier than I have ever been in my entire life. "God, I want it!" I moan. "Leg!"

I am want incarnate.

"I conceive we should be embarking regardless of this fact, Jason," she says. "It is imperative that we remove ourselves from this vicinity. To travel the highways on our two-wheeled vehicle of Japanese fabrication."

"Sounds good," I mumble, rubbing my dick into her calf, her sweet calf as soft as the softest veal. "Sounds reeeeaaaaal good..."

Starla lifts her leg and shakes me loose. I fall to the forest floor.

"Now," she says, imperiously.

"What the—?"

"I will prepare the vehicle," she says. Starla turns to the hidden bike.

"What the shit is this?" I say exactly like Dolemite in *Dolemite*. "Hump me, hairy ho!"

I leap at her back. I cling to it, grab on tightly to her hair with both hands and start humping her. Ecstasy springs eternal in my loins once more. I feel like I could come like a champ in three or four good, sexy thrusts.

"One! Two!" I shout… "Three! F—!"

But in one quick and powerful motion, Starla lifts me from her back. She plunks me up on a branch, my feet dangling ten feet off the ground, like I am some kind of doll on a shelf she's done playing with.

"Cool your jets, Jason… as they say," she says and turns her back once more to the bike. She wipes away the leaves and branches covering it.

I am enraged.

Humiliated.

I see red.

What the hell is this? "You come over here and suck my dick, and you suck it good… *Right. Now*," I say real slow and low.

I look down and see my mighty shaft sticking straight up from my lap, as if it were another branch jutting out from the main one. The Tree of Life.

Starla ignores me.

I begin to breathe heavy, my brows arched down evilly, like two black snakes. I sneer something awful.

My feelings go beyond me. It is now that the reality of my situation sets in, perhaps for the first time on our journey…

Fact: I am a naked man in a tree with an erection.

Fact: I am *somewhere*. Possibly in America. Maybe not anymore. Who knows?

Fact: I am grimy and dirty. When I have not bathed in a steaming, gross pond, that is.

Fact: There is occasionally, if not always, gray fur in my turds.

Fun fact: The family of my childhood friend is trying

to kill me. And the only thing protecting me from this homicidal bunch is the very thing that they are so desirous to get their hands on.

And the final fact: We are always moving, always on the run, exhausting ourselves to the brink of annihilation, but we have *no idea* where to. Which all adds up factually to one seriously fucked up, tender situation. There are so many unanswered questions in all this. I am privy to no real information. And I'm too balls-deep in this life-threatening situation for that. I thought I'd solved the riddle when I discovered Starla in Luke's house, but it seems now that I have only uncovered more mysteries. And then it hits me: *None of this was my idea.* I have been *kidnapped* by this monster. Stolen like a damsel from her sweet, perfect life. *My life.* My sweet, wild life of fun and cool people and Jäger whenever I feel like it, jamming on my bass with my friends in the couple of bands I'm in, bringing my low-end theory to one and all. That is what life is all about. There are limits to my wild tendencies, I am finding out. This is important: Moderation in all things. Including superseding moderation. Especially that.

That was my situation, yes. But they weren't my thoughts.

I have no thoughts. I am so unbelievably tired, horny, confused, scared, tired, horny, confused and scared (and tired) up in my tree branch that anger overrules everything else and takes supreme leadership.

No—it is more than anger.

Some beast inside me roars and bares its teeth—foams to life from the astral plane, and enters my body, hard and slicked with juices like a holy Priapus adorned with laurels. A spirit of the forest, an ancient beast from before recorded human history enters my body and consumes me up in my prison tree.

I am rage incarnate.

I am a volcano spewing the lava of hate.

And like a blob of living lava globs, I leap from the branch at Starla. Something in me wants this farce over with. Angry gravity sucks me down like a lover who wants to angrily suck their lover off. With hate.

I scream my lungs out—this disgusting caterwaul... "Christ in a crack hooouuussse!"

Starla spins, eyes wide, mouth agape. My scream has taken her by surprise. She sees the rage on my face.

I'm going to rip Starla to shreds with my bare hands! I got claws!

What!

CHAPTER FIVE
Sea Breeze[s], Sticks and Shit

Wildness. It's what it's all about, isn't it? Do you retain enough of that primal juice coursing your veins to dominate, to win, to survive? Life is a jungle. And you're welcome to it.

When I was in college I went to this keg party. There was a keg serving it up nice and frothy in the living room and they had one chilling on ice in the bathroom tub for when the first one kicked. The party was okay. Raging along brimmingly like a brimful of asha. There were some definite creamers in attendance, but I wasn't feeling it. I'd gone on a tear the month before and I was pussy-gorged, pussy-bored. I wanted more from life (whatever the hell *that* was, or could ever be—*hey* it happens) which was why I was at this weird person's house to begin with. Jazzin' up my social calendar. Anyway. Next to the CD player on the shelf in the dining room I saw was the new *Wu-Tang Forever* double album. I immediately put it on, snapping the Hootie and the Blowfish CD currently playing in half and disappearing its remains between the shelf and the wall. Then, for nearly half an hour, I stood by the CD player pressing repeat on one song and one song only: "Black Shampoo," U-God's acoustic guitar and flute-drenched paean to the tranquil, natural world, to "puffy pillow suites" and "vanilla apple heat," to "sea breeze[s], sticks and shit." I closed my eyes and nodded my head to the beat, lost in my own world. I was healing, rejuvenating my psyche for a return to myself. After about the tenth repeat the party swelled and overthrew me as DJ. Disjointed now, I wandered the throngs, looking for *something*. I was looking for me. And if I couldn't find myself, who were these other people? I went up to the roof and spit loogies down the chimney. That felt like me. I went to the host's parent's bedroom and tried on some of the mom's underwear. Put it on my head, sniffed it and put it back. That felt like me. I went to the bathroom. I peed in the trash can. It was a classic move and I felt a twinge of my old self making himself known. Then, looking down to my right, I saw the second keg in the bathtub. It occurred to me that it would be *Funny as Fuck*™ to steal this keg and bring it to another party that I knew was happening across town. Sort of like a conquering hero, I'd bust in like a wild, Dionysian god hoisting a keg like Donkey Kong on my shoulder. Yes. ME ALL THE WAY. With all haste, I went to look for the two friends I'd come with, Beefer and Scottie Tuttle. Cornering them, I told them what I wanted to do. Immediately, we concocted our nefarious plan: abscond with the potations. We swung into action (drunken) immediately. Wasting no seconds with second thoughts, we stormed the bathroom. Beefer and Tuttle hoisted the keg and I guided it out the window to the ground. The bathroom thankfully was on the first floor (I hadn't even checked). Then Beefer and Tuttle jumped through and joined me. As soon as we got it outside we realized our error. That fucker was full and heavy and slippery when wet and my car was a mile through the woods. We had to roll it. So we did. And we had rolled it halfway through the woods to the car when the hosts of the party found out what had happened: their potations had been absconded with! En masse, the hosts and their friends flowed from the house after us. We ran for it but they were fast. Beefer got away, the fat fuck, I don't know how. I never spoke to him again. Tuttle, skinny shrimplestilskin he was, got cuffed on the ear a couple times. The echoes of his high-pitched cries stabbed the Autumn woods. I ran, I bolted, laughing, singing, "Sprinkle water on chocolate, butter scotch flowers / vapor action, tropical sunshower… Dreams of peaches and cream, steam, secret spells / soft spoken gospel, Barry White acapell'…" ducking and deking branches and fists. Then I ran smack into a tree. Or what I thought was a tree, but was in fact a giant dude on the football team, a hairy linebacker named Terry Lupino. "Whoa, sticks and shit…" I fell back onto the ground. A crowd of irate drunk idiots circled above me. Then rained the fisticuffs. I was getting pummeled. Rather than die though I rose and, blind with fear and rage, leaped at the person in front of me. Coincidentally, it was the big dude Terry. He knocked me down, but now I was at his feet. I shot my face forward and bit into his hairy, gross leg. I remember his leg hair tasted like wet dog. He screamed and began raining blows upon me. I was pretty much done for, but then a car door slamming echoed through the woods and the mob stepped back. It was the parents. Sweet parental units. It was at this exact tender moment that the parents of the kids who were throwing the party decided to come home. Talk about crazy luck. We (I) might have been killed by these Neanderthals. I might no longer have been a person. The parents' car doors slammed and all the angry dudes went inside to hone their unexpressed anger like personal scrimshaw. I escaped to my car with Scottie T and went to the other party and probably found some hot snizz to snack on. I don't remember. The memory hasn't survived into the new me, though I have thought of the keg-stealing story often as something defining and personal.

Whoever the hell I am anymore, I mean. Does that define me? I tell this story as a definition of who I am as a wild person in this tale—but is it me? Is that action me? How can an action be someone? Self-help gurus and U.S. Marines TV ads always say this: Your actions define you. But I am only an anatomical body. A person is, and can only ever be, a meat-drenched skeleton. Actions are things that exist only accidentally on a timeline.

So if we aren't our actions, what are we? Are we our thoughts? Our emotions? Our memories? Our two possibilities: our potential for good, our potential for bad?

Identity is a slippery thing.

*What the *fuck* are we?*

One time, as an agent of light and joy, I tried to steal a keg from a generic keg party and agents of darkness hunted me through the woods in stereotypical fashion. Now, as I chase Starla through the woods, am I an agent of darkness? Agents of darkness never believe themselves to be agents of darkness. They always see themselves as the keg: insulted purity.

Yes, as I hunt my soon-to-be-slaughtered lover through hill and dale, I am pure. I am the keg gone wild—a dead weight of sloshing possibility.

I am a vessel of primal juice.

I am wild.

Chapter Six
Dick Prickles

Starla whimpers and scampers away. I fall from the tree like a meteor: angry, with a hot butt.

"No!" Starla screams.

"Yesss!"

I make a mad lunge at her. She jumps out of the way. I slam into a tree. This enrages me more. I see only red. There are red trees. Red leaves. A red moon. A red sasquatch backing up away from me with fear in her red eyes.

"The wildness, it is in you!" Starla says.

"Yesss…" I hiss, crouching like a demon.

I spring up and sprint after her. Starla turns tail and makes for the deep woods. She pounds the ground away from me, but I am relentless. She bounds into the darkness, but I am after her. She can run but she can't hide. I can smell her smell. Always, anywhere. My skin is bristling. I can feel it harden to the cool air as I run like a cheetah after her.

"No, my pet!" Starla yells as she runs. "This is not you! This is not you!"

"Oh, it's me!" I gristle with my whistle. It's all I can get out, my face scrunched up.

And really, there are no words. I feel the anger course

through me. The murderous delight of the wild jungle. Pure. I am a fucking animal now. You're not gonna fuck me? Well I'll fuck you.

"Please! You must bathe!"

"Ha!"

She disappears into the dark but her smell—her barnyard odor—mixes now with the pheromonal skunkweed of fear sparkling from her glands and there is no way I could lose her. I could track this prey to the ends of the earth.

And it is this fear of hers that propels me forward, inspires me to kill her—to kill her and be free of her. Fear is an asking.

Somehow I am faster now. Am I running on four legs? I catch up to Starla and leap at her. She screams, more helpless and high-pitched than I've ever heard from her deep throat. My fingernails claw into her back. Starla whelps. She ducks and I go flying into a thicket of pricker bushes, handfuls of her hair in my fists. The thorns tear into my skin. I look down and see blood on my body. My blood. Or is that hair? Hairy blood? Swaying in the moonlight by its own power? I laugh. It feels great.

Far away, in the dark Starla is moving away. She speaks, almost whispering, though I can hear her as if I were next to her: "It is my wildness… You must bathe, my lover. Please, this is not you."

I'm up again. Moving. Bleeding. I have a boner. It slaps against my stomach in the dark like a truncheon.

This is very much me. The most *me* I've ever been.

For half an hour I track her. An hour. Two… Deeper we go into the forest. I hear no trace of the highway. I snout and sniff. It must be for miles. I don't keep track. All

I know is the circle of trees around me and the lurid scent of a sasquatch luring me on. A vulture brain. An owl brain. A wolf brain. My brain is all predator.

Minutes or hours—the cycles of time are lost to me now—go by. I stop to rub my cock against the rough bark of a tree. I defecate. I urinate. I lift my leg over rocks, trees, fallen logs.

After a time of a million thundering heartbeats I come to a ridge and look down the other side. There is the prey. There is Starla down at the bottom. She is crouched, her back to me. Probably exhausted. Given up. The chase has tired her out. Good. My heart quickens. My mouth salivates. My dick prickles.

There is light all around her. She is glowing somehow. This does not concern me.

My chest yearns for a howl. I long to lift my throat to the skies and unleash a howl such as would shake the angels from Heaven.

But instinct tells me that stealth is required. Only the stealth of a cat o' prey will work here.

I am able to keep from howling, but I cannot contain myself. I sprint at the beast. When I get my claws on her, I will feel alive.

So be it.

The hill is steep. I barrel down it, bounding like a bear, with eyes of the tiger. My heart races! I feel the death-joy of the master. The prey spins, I see a look in her eyes… surprise, maybe… but not the fear I long for.

What is this?

I am upon her now. I can't stop. My flesh-death is upon her. I leap onto her body. She acquiesces to my power. We tumble onward… me forward… the prey backward…

And suddenly everything is different.

CHAPTER SEVEN
On Like Donkey Kong

Surprised! is the word.

I splash into water with Starla, end over end. Instantly the heat, the rage, the Animal Fuck-Quest™ is washed away.

I am me again: good old Jason Fields, naked boy extraordinaire.

"What in the world!" I shout.

We are standing in a pond. Or, I am. Starla sits in it like a tub. The water is dark and cool, edged all around with lily pads. The pond is alone in the dark forest. How much of America is undeveloped like this? How many of these bathing places are there? It's so easy to think that everywhere in this country is development and suburban sprawl—soon, but not yet.

I look up. "Oh, moon," I say. "Glow… you, glow-ing, glow, up. Up… I mean, when *I* up…"

"Yes, pet," Starla says.

She washes me down. Collects pond water in her paws and pours it over my head. I let it happen. The heat dissipates like a window thrown open on my soul—cool water extinguishing my soul on fire like a burning schoolhouse.

"You backlit by moon… dumb brain, my, mine saw…

animal, ugh… was the big round moon, like, reflecting on the surface of this, um… water place thing…"

"Sshhhh…" she says and laves my body with her paws, two scabrous yet gentle luffas, cooling me, calming me.

"Ahhhh…"

She's right. I should shush. Talking is hurting. It just feels good to be and to get washed.

The water and her touch relaxes me.

Eventually though, the madness comes back to me—the memory of it. That kind of madness you can't forget. It comes back to me like a dream comes back later in the day out of nowhere.

"Oh! Starla, I don't know what got into me. I'm so sorry. I am ashamed. You've been nothing but a peach to me. A sweet Georgia peach."

"I do."

"You do what?"

"I know what came over you," Starla says. "It is my greatest fear and it has come true."

"I was just mad is all. Blue-balled, you know? Just horny. We've been out here so long in the woods. It's just like… *grrrr*… ya know?"

"That is true, pet. But that is not the reason I am cognizant of fear." She runs her hand along the base of my back. She cups my buttocks in the water and a thrill runs through my loins like a river runs through it.

"Mmm," I say. "Nice."

She eyeballs me and stops rubbing. Apparently this bum-frottage was by accident. Bummer.

"Do you think you can walk now without the rage overcoming you? It is distant to our vehicle. Perhaps we can acquire a new one in this vicinity. I do not possess knowledge of our location. But we have many miles to go before rendezvous. That is obvious now." She is saying all this with a patina of sadness I can't explain.

"Sure, I mean. But what is it? Your fear, I mean. Why is it your biggest fear?"

"You have the same rage I have now. I know this rage. Somehow you have obtained my rage inside of your body. The rage of the animal. Like a virus."

"Shit. What's wrong with that?"

"Everything."

"But now we're closer, Starla. We're closer than ever!"

"Do you not see? I approve of your presence in my life as a mate precisely because you are not like me. I am desirous of your prostrations because you are different—because you are a human being of the planet Earth. Somehow you have gotten the bug that plagues my systems. It is frightening to me for the reason that I do not know how. I have made every precaution."

"I was born wild, Starla. I'm a wild dude. I like to party. Been that way since forever, since I was a kid rippin' wheelies on my neighbor's lawns and hopping the river behind the Junior High School like Evel frankfurtin' Knievel. Always had an intense dislike for all the normals, all the Norms and Normettes. It's like, take me away from the norm, all that normal human stuff, Norman. Norm! (Cheers)"

"I need you to remain human."

"Why? For sasquatch reasons? For space reasons?"

"I am inculcating this word *wild* of yours. How it is used and expressed. I believe I understand it now. But it does not mean that you acquire the wildness of another. It means you stay yourself and experience the wildness of the other. This is not to mention it is an ailment common to my people, and not safe for your anatomy, but what if I became or acted more human? What if I were just another little, hairless humanoid? Would that be wild? If you became like me you would cease to be wild, to be *other*, to me, but also to yourself. Hence, I would no longer be wild to *you*."

"Hmmm… Pretty deep, lady," I say and begin playing with her hair. She does not stop me.

"I need you to be you," she says. "And I will be as deep as you need me to be."

"Intriguing."

I step closer to her in the water. I press my naked skin to her body, her body like a soaked bath mat, deliciously so. Maybe because I've scared myself with my own anger I am suddenly more tender, more loving towards her. Crisis breeds infatuation, that kind of thing. "I'll be me…" I gyrate against her. "I'll be me if you be you."

Starla coos and clicks.

The pond ripples the reflection of starlight all around us like a flurry of lightning bugs.

I step into her and she enfolds me in her huge, hairy arms. Her wet breasts weigh down on the top of my head.

Emotions are high.

It's on like Donkey Kong.

CHAPTER EIGHT
Bums Beyond Belief

Dost thou seek literary representations of the pleasures twixt flesh and fur, astute and curious reader? For sooth, it is all here in this twisty text and more…

I caress Starla's front, the elegant and shapely pelt that knows the ways of love. With idle fingers, I stroke up and down her stomach, smirking a sexy smirk.

She's a big lady and knows how to please a man. Starla's bosoms heave, she shimmies her round hips under the water and I feel her legs spread ever so slightly. She licks her simian lips. Her throat clicks. And her velvety coat strokes me in return.

I stopped questioning many days and many more miles ago how her hair could do this. Whether from ancient woods magic or intergalactic science, it doesn't even matter. It's *too good.* You don't question the means when the results are your wang getting the Royal-Penis-is-Clean-Your-Highness treatment so hard it's like you're the Queen of England but for glands and not englands.

"Your hair is loving me up proper, what you say, Hammer, proper."

"Very delightful, delightful human male unit…" Starla looks down at me with sultry eyes. Her long eyelashes flutter, demure. Her dimples widen like crescent moons. Like Fred Astaire and Ginger Rogers her two fingers dance up and down my back. The pond water is cool and I shiver. Not without pleasure.

"What should we do to celebrate?" I ask, my voice a mere murmur blending with the air around us. I slide my hands down her stomach into the water. I find her hips and trace the lines inward to her feminine center.

"Cele—brate?" she says, her voice going up.

"Our getting back together. Our first fight. That's big," I say. "What are we gonna do?" And then my fingers dip quickly to the top of Starla's sasquatch pussy. She breathes in quickly. Shocked. "Let me in there. I want to celebrate in there. The VIP room."

"I am conceptualizing," Starla says.

"Oh yeah?"

"It involves the recent past."

"Oh yeah?" I mumble. I'm not really paying attention. I'm occupied with her clitoris, rubbing her luscious little bump in cross-patterns. Flicking it with my thumbs. Pearl One. Flick Two. I am a weaver of dreams.

"It involves trees."

I snap out of my Bigfoot clitoris-induced hypnosis. "Trees?" I say.

"Affirmative."

And with that Starla picks me up and leaps from the pond. The water comes off her like a waterfall. The air is chilly. The air is silly.

"But don't you need to cool down?" I say, cupped in her body. "Water… Heat… The song of your people…"

"I am no longer in estrus," Starla says.

"What the what? Estrus?"

"My *time*," she says. "I am no longer what you humans call 'in heat.'"

"Oh? Does that mean—I mean… you're not… you know… horny? You don't want…? Is that why you didn't want to go in for the deuce with me right before I went psycho? Deuce Bigalow Male Gigolo?"

"It is not like that, Jay Jason. My *physiology* is not like that, I mean to express. It is simply not my time. My time requires cool-down periods to prevent overheating and damage to my system. I am extra-concupiscent during my time, that is true, but it does not mean that I am not willing or able to perform sexual congress with my carnal systems at other times."

"Nice."

Starla carries me through the woods. We come to a tree. It is large.

"Hush now, let us not speak with audible words, but with our bodily units and parcels."

"Okay, baby."

Starla hoists my body like a doll and plops me on a branch again, my crotch as high as her head. Instantly my dick springs to life.

"The tree of life," I say, legs dangling playfully. "Nice." My dick hardens harder than any old branch could ever hope to be hard. Dumbass fucking trees, nice try.

Starla bends forward and takes me into her mouth. Her lips are soft and warm. They squeeze tightly around my cock. Like her body hair, it's as if her lips have a mind of their own. They wobble and wiggle this way and that, undulating across the head of my dick and down the shaft in magical waves of pleasure.

My toes curl. I tilt my head back and I let out a moan

up into the leaves. "Ooooohh woogie woogie woogie wooooo…" I moan, almost falling backward off the branch.

Starla laughs and keeps me from falling by locking her lips around my dick. I laugh too.

Everything feels too good not to laugh. We'd come through the eye of a needle. At that precise moment, I had no idea things were about to get seriously weird and more fucked up than a rodeo in a retirement home, but we'd survived my stupid wild outburst and here we two were back living the high life once again like Steve Winwood fisting two cans of High Life.

Starla deslurps her mouth from my mighty branch with trails of saliva, like when you pull up a slice of pizza and the cheese just gets longer and longer. My dick sproi-oi-oi-oings back and forth.

"Come," she says. Nay, commands.

"By myself?" I ask. "Just like, by *thinking* of it? Wow… what an idea…" I say. I try to think sexy thoughts and make myself jizz. It's kind of hot. I think of wonderful women, of bums beyond belief. It's sunset over the desert dunes, there's a harem full of women in robes with delicate filigree, like slaves and such—imported from all over the globe, given as tribute to me, some oligarch's spoiled son. It's raining, Greenwich Village, 1962, a young ingénue in a mackintosh huddles close to me in the doorway of a shoe repair shop. It's the future, post-apocalyptic, drones in the sky, roving zombie hordes hard on my heel, a young mother in a skintight futuristic outfit and with dark, supple eyes reaches her hand to me from the closing door of a fallout shelter, closing, closing, closing so, so, so tight, will I get there in time? Women, babes, chicks. I think of entering a lady, any lady, *all* ladies, of opening them up like the door to a harem tent or a shoe repair shop or a fallout shelter and of licking to life joys untold between their legs and the ecstasies undiscovered within…

"No, that is not what I meant, human male lover," Starla says and jumps up on the tree next to me, folded over on her haunches like a Queen of the Apes. "Come. I want you to meet my people."

Chapter Nine

Randy of the Redwoods '94 Remix

We ascend through the leaves.

"I have more pertinent knowledge to divulge," Starla says.

"Preach on, girlie goo."

"I have *many* times. My time of estrus is simply one of these times. It is important, affirmative, but it is merely an exordium, a prelim, to a more important time: the time of connection and commingling."

"Nice."

We reach to the top of the tree. The trunk is thin and the tree sways with our weight. A gentle wind buffets and tickles us. The view is astounding. Dark forest marches in every direction with a canopy of stars overhead and a big, full moon smiles down on everything with its pale blue light.

"Commingling is a time well-suited for rendezvous, pet," Starla says.

"Is this it?" I ask. "Is this the rendezvous? Are we really Audi 5000?" My spine tingles with anticipation. I look up at the stars, trying to find the one Starla pointed out, but naturally I can't find it. It's all so very bracing—to point to a star and *actually* reach it. Will a starship explode through the atmosphere and hover above us, pulling us up in a tractor beam? Or will we have to walk up a gangplank, like in ET?

"Perhaps," she says. "I feel it is so."

Maybe because of this anticipation, our yearnings are enlivened—spring to life like a stop-motion video of flowers growing from the soil.

And like a magnet we are drawn into one another. We hug. We kiss. I go down on Starla and eat out her hairy pussy like a man dying of starvation.

Up in the treetops, I realize, we are truly in our element—on a swaying intermediate zone between the forest and the stars. I mean this is what it's all about, isn't it? This is where space gorillas make their love.

Starla's pubic hair curls around my ears. It tickles and I giggle. I jab my tongue at her clitoris, lick it up and down. Starla's wraps her legs around me. Down below her, I dry hump what leaves my dick can reach. The wind picks up. Her hair ripples everywhere. She moans as if wounded. I'm breaking her down to her sexy essence. To the nub of her womanhood—the woman inside the woman where she is realer than a RealPlayer™ media file.

"The time… has come…" Starla mumbles through her delight.

"Come then…" I say into the lovely moist pelt before me, dripping with out-of-this-world juices.

"The time… *Oh*… coming…" She says, quivering.

"Come my lady, come, come my lady…" I sing, licking her wonderfully wet gibbon-like pussy. I can feel her body shaking. "You're my butterfly, sugar baby…"

"I mean…" she moans in ribbons of jellied tones, "the time for… *Commmuuuuu-uuuunicationnnnn…*"

Then I touch an important sex-nerve with my tongue.

I must have. Because she lets out a shriek. It is nearly as loud as one of those "shrieks of her people" she does that knock me out like LL Cool J's mama. But Starla is smart. She squeezes her massive thighs tighter to the sides of my head and blocks out the sound. It is a sexy, hairy soundproofing that Electric Lady Studios would be psyched to insulate their sound booths with. *(Note to self: Business idea? —Ed.)* I only feel the vibrations of her sonic boom in my torso.

It is becoming hard to breath though, trapped between her legs. It's hot. And bothered.

I put my hand where my tongue was and I slide my head out from her thighs. "Does it feel good, butterfly?" I ask, looking up into Starla's face.

But Starla is far away.

Her head is back, looking straight up into the night sky. I continue my rubbings of her ruggings, with forefinger, thumbs—all the fingers get into it, really, like a basketball team running a triangle offense. Her lips tremble with pleasure. Her whole body shakes.

I've seen enough female orgasms to know that hers is coming fast.

With furious fingers I guide Starla to her apex of joy. She shakes. Her body vibrates in tune with the universe. The tree sways in a wide arc now. A low rumble starts inside her, down in her belly. It gains momentum. Any minute now, Starla is going to come. She is going weak—her giantesses' body, as big as a mountain, trembles as if shook by an earthquake deep within.

By turns, her legs holding us to the tree clench and go weak, clench and go week. I hear a million little bones inside her cracking and whirring like tiny machines as she curls to the pleasure.

One more stroke… another…

Starla climaxes and the treetop spins in a wide circle over the forest like a ride at a county fair.

I open my mouth with admiration and admire how her body seems to glow. An amber light emanates from her very hairy body. Her little hairs glow amber and gold as if each were a little candle, holding back darkness as one. I see her energy. Her very soul illuminates the darkness, and opens itself to me.

And then it happens.

Starla leans back and opens her mouth incredibly wide. For nearly a full minute she inhales—powerful as a jet intake. Then, in one great sweep of spirit, she releases a howl to the heavens. The howl is of a booming volume and power I have never heard. It is gigantic and seemingly nuclear-powered.

Unlike her many other simian shrieks this does not cause me pain or pierce my ear drums. But I am hypnotized dumb by it. It is a rich, low sound, deeper and growlier than the deepest bass—deeper than dropped D—deeper than the low B on a five string bass, if you can believe that.

I feel the sound in my loins. The howl is a song. My dick sways back and forth as if enraptured by the tune. My insides effervesce and mellow.

She continues to boom.

It's almost as if I can *see* the sound of her sasquatch howl. It is a dark tube of sound, an onyx fiber-optic cable undulating upward. I see it travel up into the atmosphere, the stratosphere and beyond. I see the howl shoot out into the solar system and disappear among the stars.

"Whoa-oh," I manage to say. And like I'm in a pack of dogs or something, her howl unlocks a deep need inside me: I want to howl too, and exactly like in that Kafka story about dogs, "I believed that great things were going on around me of which I was the leader and to which I must lend my voice…I was completely under their spell…filled with the premonition of great things."

I pull myself from the hot zone of her snatch and crawl up her chest, hand-over-hand like on a fireman's ladder.

Here it comes…

"Howoooooooooooooooolllllllllllllll!!!!!!!" I howl into the vacant reaches of space. "Hoooooowwwwwwwooooooooolllllllllll!" The feeling is beyond freeing. I am freer than the Declaration of Independence.

My treble joins Starla's bass and we rock it. We rock whatever it is we're doing. I howl from the deepest, darkest part of my diaphragm, and ululate like a beast.

And then, whatever it is we're doing, it does it.

Our howls pierce the night. It explodes. The sky opens up like a ball of fire. All around us is light. A light and a blasting, electrical hum. I can barely see Starla from the glare. Everything is white. I am blind.

Um?

Is this supposed to be happening? It doesn't feel good, actually. Maybe it's because I've never experienced interplanetary sound-travel or something, but it *really* doesn't feel good at all.

Adding to this impression of unpleasantness is Starla—she is screaming. Her bassy howl comes to a shuddering stop, replaced by a shattering screech. She screams as if in pain. I flinch. Starla flinches too. She unhooks her legs from the tree and tries to cover her eyes with them.

"Oh no!"

We fall. We fall through the branches and the ungodly bright light. It's hard to tell which is worse.

I scream like a little girl and Starla grunts like a trucker. The branches crack and the leaves crackle, they snap like broken bones as we plow through them.

In a horrible heartbeat we are at the bottom of the tree. Gravity, you can get the deez. Starla catches a thick branch in the lumbar and bounces one way. I fly another.

"Ugh, oof…!" I hit the ground rolling, nail my head on a rock and smash into another tree with my shoulder.

I'm down, but not out. I'm dazed, but not contused. Well, maybe I am. I lurch up onto my elbow and look for Starla. I see her blur scrambling into the dark woods away from the blinding light. She looks over her shoulder. Fear—guilt or something—in her eyes.

Is she abandoning me?

This is terrible. I try to speak. "Star…" I croak. Speaking… it's difficult—a strange feeling compared to what joyful noise we were hooting not seconds before. "Star…" Darkness crowding the edges of my vision. If I could only say her name. "Star…" is all I manage. I slump back down.

"Hi!" a chipper voice says suddenly to my right. "Are you okay? Stars? Are you seeing stars? And aren't *you* a randy boy! Reminds me of Woodstock '94, naked out here in the woods like this!"

CHAPTER TEN
Surface Tension of a Cheese Wheel

"That was quite some noise," the chipper voice says.

I can stand. Sort of. I lean against the nefarious tree that whaled me in the shoulder. I do a body check. I'm bruised in a bajillion places, but nothing seems broken except my spirit. Do I have a boner? I don't know. Probably. I'd been blue-balled to the nth for the nth time this lengthy trip. An engorged chub swings down like a side o' beef from my full-frontal nudity and casts a monster of a shadow across the trees. The shadow is actually so big that I think it's my Conquering Hero coming back for me. "Star..." I say, hopeful, on tender wings.

"You keep saying *star*," the voice says again.

It's getting to the point where I should probably investigate this voice, I think to myself in my foghat.

I turn.

What the?

It's a midget. A female midget!

I laugh. I don't mean to. Against my better judgment, I laugh. I mean, the sight is just so surprising after all that's happened out here in the middle of the woods. "Well, what the heck!" I exclaim. "What are you doing out here, li'l lady?"

"Little?" the woman says. She has a round face, with rosy cheeks and a large nose and nostrils. She is not unattractive, in a human sort of way. She wears all sorts of flouncy, flowing clothes, see-through rainbow scarves and whatnot. A lot of flair, probably meant to hide the older-lady body beneath. She's a hippie—a wiccan type—with horsey, chestnut hair. (That's nice and animal-esque, anyway, my brain nudges.) "Honey, it's been a *long* time since anyone called *me* little."

"Oh…" I trail off, light dawning on Marblehead.

And then it hits me. I'd been with Starla, my giant, alone in the woods so long that I'd forgotten what regular people looked like! Doy! My scale was off!

"I'm sorry," I mumble. "It's… the woods… I…"

"Well, I suppose anyone with something *that* size," she says, and makes googly eyes down at my crotch, "has the right to call anyone little. Sheeze. Is there a tribe of you back out here? An entrepreneur could make a killing setting up a little, ah, 'comfort tent,' something for the ladies besides $8 bottles of water."

And then, as if testing the surface tension of a cheese wheel, this middle-aged hippie woman reaches down and pokes the top of my engorged dick with her index finger. Coincidentally, or so simultaneously that it feels like fortune, the dazzling light that had flooded the woods and knocked Starla and I from our tree shuts off.

The darkness is deafening.

My dick wobbles; I shake my head. "What, uh? Who are you? What was that light?" I say in the darkness.

"Name's Athena. Athena Lily Diller. But you can call me 'Long Hair Don't Care Sister of Wounded Birds Mystic

Poetess Singer of Mountains Songs and Imbiber of the Kindest Herbal Supplements' for short. Or Tina if you like. P.S. Was that you making that sonic joy I heard?" she asks.

"Are you a Hobbit?" I venture, still musty-brained. "What the hell're you doing out here in the middle of nowhere?"

"Middle of nowhere? What are you, one of the Hansons? And anyway, kiddo, we're fifteen seconds from Baltimore. Columbia, Maryland. Ever hear of it?"

"Say whaaa?"

"Industry talk. Come on, big boy. Let's get you some water and a B12 shot at the medical tent. Should be set up already."

Tina unwraps one of her scarves and spins it around my hips, sheathing my manhood. Then she takes my hand and walks back towards where the light came from. Not really sure why I do it, but I don't fight it. I go with her.

"Was back checking the electrical when I heard, what do you call it, that song of yours? You a gate crasher or something? Man, you guys get more desperate every year. It's nuts."

I don't really have answers for these questions. My brain is an acorn. My feet do the following.

Quickly, the trees grow more sparse. The woods suddenly seem manicured and not wild. Ahead of us is an expanse of space. Maybe a field sloping down. My acorn does not register what I see. But somewhere, somewhere deep within my cerebral cortex, I register what I hear. Suddenly there is sound in a dark spot past the field. The sound is a song. A song begins to play. A song of angels doing the wet and sticky in my ears.

It is my life the song plays.

My destiny.

Blue and yellow stage lights come up on a band. I can't believe my eyes or ears. It's 311. And they're playing "Down" to an empty amphitheater nestled in the darkness down past the sloping field. It's 311 and they're playing the post-grunge, rap-rock party groove anthem "Down"—probably my most favorite tune in the world—to me and me alone. It feels like rescue. I fall to my knees.

"Where… the hell am I?" I ask, agape. "Heaven? Am I dead?"

"You don't know where you are do you? Man, you *are* messed up. It *is* heaven, though… a little bit of it, anyway," Tina says.

"Huh?"

"Welcome to the Lilith Fair, big boy."

CHAPTER ELEVEN
Chapter (Three) Eleven

"What's going on? Is this a free concert?" I ask and walk towards the stage—float on air, really.

"Thinkin' we should head over to the medi-tent," Tina the hippie, the horsey mystical mountain herb lady says, and hooks my elbow with hers. "Stocks are low. The CSNY2K Tour came through here last weekend and the old farts were dropping like flies, but I know where the extra B12's are. I was a nurse a million lifetimes ago before I joined the dark side and became a promoter," she says and laughs a horsey, hippie laugh, Hot to Trot.

"How come no one's here?" I look around, confused.

311's patented blend of philosophy-influenced hip-hop and hard-edged funk rock echoes all over the vacant amphitheater and lawn. My head shakes at this travesty, then nods to the beat.

"Hey, what's your name, anyway, big boy?"

"Jason F—. Jason."

"They're just sound checking, Jason F. Jason. The festival is tomorrow."

I take this, as well as the last dope strains of the "Down" outro riff, in.

Tina points me towards a row of tents off to the side

of the lawn and after a few seconds and some communication between the band and a sound guy, the bass player, P-Nut, starts riffing a sweet bass line. I've never heard it. It's chill though, and gets me where it counts in the bass place. I noodle across the lawn, the grass massaging my burnt toes, to the sweet bass lickage. But Nick—Nick Hexum, guitarist and lead singer—doesn't seem to like it. Nick cuts in suddenly with the acidic, angular intro to "Come Original." It's the band's new hit currently tearing the Billboard charts a new one.

We reach the tent. Tina sits me down on a bench. She rifles through a cabinet and I listen to "Come Original," smiling ear to ear, nodding my head.

"Well this is a treat," I say.

Tina pulls out a needle and and gives me a shot. After a few moments I feel its effects. 311 had already brought me back round to the land of living, but the B12 doesn't hurt.

"Now, are you going to tell me what was making that noise I heard out there?" Tina asks.

She places a small stool in front of me and sits down on it. I look at her and see she's eyeballing the bulge below her scarf in my lap. It takes me a minute to realize that she probably heard Starla and me howling to the moon.

"Noise?" I say. No need to make myself seem more cuckoo than I already am. I'll just listen to the band sound check, I think, and skedaddle back to Starla and get the hell out of here. Lilith Fair? No thanks. Even *with* 311.

"Was like nothing I'd ever heard. You *had* to have heard it out there. Big, weird, wobbly sound?" Tina asks and laughs. She taps my knee with a teeny-tiny rubber hammer and it reflects forward. "Good," she says. After a brief moment she runs her finger around my knee, then rests her hand on it. She looks up into my eyes. "Was it you? Come on, tell me…"

My johnson rouses, but I shake my head. I'm not giving up the goods. It was our private, mystical love song, and though it could probably attract hordes of people to join in our lovemaking, cure cancer and bring peace to the Middle East, I wanted it all for me. "No," I reply.

"Hmm, well, what are you—"

"The festival," I say. "The Fair, I mean. You know. Gettin' in free."

Tina frowns. Before she can say anything more though, there's a commotion on stage. A bunch of un-chill sounds happen.

We both look and see P-Nut talking to Nick. It seems tense. Nick says something and P-Nut goes over to another microphone. "This is goddamned bullshit!" P-Nut yells and throws his bass down violently onto the stage. Nasty feedback that reminds me of Starla's wild screeching assaults the empty fairgrounds.

The band stops playing. They all commiserate with one another. Nick shakes his head and walks around. This is all very interesting to me.

"…so sick of this. Any other bass players out there—as if?" Nick says into his microphone, offhand. The frustration is evident in his voice. He seems tired.

"Are they—is he serious?" I ask Tina.

"How should I know? Though this is the Lilith Fair, hon. *Anything's* possible."

I take my leave of the tent. Tina's wanting hand remains unengaged. I walk towards the stage across the lawn. When I get to the back of the covered seats of the amphitheater I shout through cupped hands, "I can hang, yo!"

The band is milling around on stage. Nick hears me and walks up to the front. He covers his eyes. "Who said that?" he says into the mic.

I speedwalk down an aisle, rainbow groin-scarf flapping. "Me!" I shout. "I can rock it. Dude, I know all your songs! You guys are one of my favorite bands of all time!" I don't wait for an invitation. I walk past a couple of aghast tech dudes, a few burly roadies, climb on stage and pick up the offended git-box. "The bass tabs anyway," I say and slide the strap around my shoulder.

311 stare at me. No one moves. Maybe it's because I'm basically nude and filthy and bruised and I just fell out of a tree, but whatever. I start slapping that thing like it's a bad girl. I really go to town on it—Town and Gown a medley of all the 311 licks I know. All the hits, some deep cuts. I do it for a full five minutes, riffin' like David Ruffin. I guess I know more than I thought I knew.

Nick laughs and smiles—big blond-haired, blue-eyed rock god that he is. He holds up a hand. I stop. "Okay, okay," he says, looking around at his bandmates. "We get it." And then he does it: He launches into "Come Original" again.

This time, though, the bass player doesn't have a hissy fit. This time the bass player locks in with the drummer like a twin, riding the beat like a gnarly wave. My heart swells. Just to jam with these dudes is intense. I even pop off a few sinister leg-lifts à la P-Nut, but I try not to overdo it—need to maintain my own identity. But it doesn't feel real. This whole thing. Reality warbles when you're on stage. It's funny… All the weird shit I've been doing the past month and *this* is the thing that doesn't feel real.

We plow through the whole new album. We even do a couple covers: "Miserable" by Lit and soulDecision's "Faded" (me doing the rap!). I keep on top of it all, especially the songs I don't know. I just wing it. I feel the music deep down and go wild with it. Even if the notes aren't the real notes, the notes are *mine* and therefore correct and killer.

Thirty minutes later we're done. (Suzanne Vega has been waiting in the wings to sound check this whole time making petulant faces at us.) I'm sweaty and smiling and back in love with life. I'm in the moment. I'm myself.

"Wow. Who the hell *are* you?" Nick says.

"Me? Jason. I'm Jason Fields."

"Okay, Jason Fields. You're in."

"I'm in what?"

"Well, certainly not a pair of pants," SA Martinez says, stepping from behind his turntable rig with a sly grin twisting his goatee. "But. Yeah, you're in. You're in 311. If you want, dude."

"Whaaaaaaaat!!!!!"

And I scorch out a howl Starla would (and my new bandmates can) be proud of.

CHAPTER TWELVE

Stupid, Old Boring Noodlers Singing Siren Songs Full of Noodles

I wasn't lying about 311 being one of my favorite bands. Whether you think it ironic or not, they made the cut.

The first house I lived in after college had a subscription to Rolling Stone *in situ.* Someone named Dong L. McBong had the magazine sent to the house and they forgot to cancel it or do address forwarding or whatever when they moved. Either that or they died and Rolling Stone was draining Dong's parents' credit cards unbeknownst. Happens all the time.

Anyway, since I fancied myself a musician I would peruse this industry glad rag whenever it dirtied my doorstep. *Howling mad* is how I usually ended up when I finished. Some manufactured robot like Britney Spears would get the full Bob-Dylan-ingénue cover treatment, all their personality peccadilloes respected and cataloged—meanwhile a true musician like Squarepusher gets 2.06 out of 5 stars and a sour 400-word critique by a self-loathing reviewer. I always hated those lists they did too: like, Top 50 Guitarists, or the 100 Greatest Artists of All-Time. They always back-loaded the thing. Like Jimi Hendrix would be neck-and-neck with the lead guitarist from Dishwalla just because Dishwalla had a CD out three minutes ago and a record exec was applying moisturizer to David Fricke's short and curlies. It's the fallacy of currency. To assume that things presently happening are inherently better than what came before. (Equally bad, I suppose are those dickjobs who only like "classic rock" and things that are already sacrosanct and ensconced. What timidity. What aural cowardice. Eat a dick, David Fricke.) Also, Jimi Hendrix always won Best Guitarist. *Wow.* What a stretch. What investigative journalism went into that *coup de foudre*?

So it was after one of these howlers, and a heaping helping hunk of my roommate Ratboy's schwag, that I sat down with pen and paper and wrote out my own list: The One Hundred Best Bands of All-Time—focus on the "bands" part. Which is why you won't see Johnny Cash on here, or Bob Dylan or Elton John (who wouldn't have made it anyway—I hate them all). The history of Rock & Roll is the history of bands. Mini-armies joining their misaligned energies to create a nervous, hectic sound. It's the lattice of dissonance that uplifts us, not solo artists with all the answers.

I tried to be fair. I tried to be timeless. And you know what?

I succeeded.

So here it is, Rolling Stone and all you other so-called music maggy mags. The 100 Best Bands of All-Time. The DEFINITIVE LIST… You Dong L. McBong-washers.

1. Led Zeppelin — Led Zep first. Beatles second. Only because the Beatles weren't a true rock band. They were a boy band, which is essentially a collection of solo artists. (Look at their contract. Every member had to have at least one

song where they sung lead—explaining George and Ringo's inexplicable early inclusions.) In terms of who did what and what went where, Bobbie Plant & The Lead Balloons were the consummate band's band. Everyone's role in the group dissonating with pure power. Women wanted them; men wanted to be them. And mystery and stairways and pan-flutes and riffage—pure dissonant magic of the magi.

2. The Beatles — Inevitable shitstorm to follow when this list goes public. David Fricke, I know how you feel, buddy. And here are their solo careers in order of importance post-Beatles.
    a. John
    b. George
    c. Paul
    d. Ringo
3. Huey Lewis and the News
    a. The News
    b. Huey Lewis
    c. Ray Parker Jr. haha
4. AC/DC — And the no-brainer of the century (and the other guy would surely agree):
    a. Bon Scott
    b. Other guy
5. ZZ Top — Listen to the early stuff. The early stuff and the later stuff and the latest stuff. Get your wig burnt, son. The dissonance at the atomic heart of this group begins and ends with the fact that the one guy in the band without a beard is named Frank Beard.
6. Pixies
    a. Kim Deal
    b. Frank Black
7. The Funk Brothers — Otherwise known as the backup band for all the Motown hits. James Jamerson, Pistol Allan, Earl Van Dyke, etc. I'm

not even going to stoop to rank them individually. They're all number one. Watch *Standing in the Shadows of Motown* or lose my number.

8. Gentle Giant
9. Outkast
    a. Big Boi
    b. Andre 3000
10. The Commodores — this band is fire in the flesh. All their deep cuts cut deep as a Rambo Knife. (Unlike Queen who have only hits, for instance, and no deep cuts—just fluffy filler.) Every song is a funk jam that funks you in the funking place. FYI:
    a. The rest of the Commodores
    b. Lionel Richie
11. Lynyrd Skynyrd
12. The Meters
13. Bachman-Turner Overdrive
    a. Bachman
    b. Turner
    c. Overdrive
14. Black Sheep
15. Black Sabbath
16. Black Flag
17. The JB's — should probably rate all the bands. Such a wide variety over such a long time.
18. The Byrds
19. ~~Guns 'n Roses~~ Nirvana — the torch has been passed.
20. ~~The Neville Brothers~~ Built to Spill — the torch has been passed.
21. Guns 'n Roses
22. Wu-Tang Clan
    a. Method Man
    b. Ol' Dirty Bastard
    c. U-God

   d. GZA
   e. Cappadonna
   f. Raekwon
   g. Ghostface Killah
   h. Inspectah Deck
   i. Masta Killa
   j. RZA

23. Judas Priest is the baddest because of *Heavy Metal Parking Lot*, otherwise… who comes next? That's right. Iron Maiden.
24. ~~Electric Light Orchestra — this is not a band, this is a fun-sound circus of goofy, gooey neon feeling. So, I don't know.~~ Unrest and Air Miami
25. Public Enemy
26. The Kinks
27. The Jimi Hendrix Experience — Listen up pal, if it weren't for the Experience part, you wouldn't even be on here, so. Recognize.
28. The Beach Boys — Not a band, I know. Sort of a Jacuzzi full of warm, massaging sound. Coincidentally, the first time I visited L.A. I sat in a hot tub at a friend's house by myself and looked up at the hills and I really *felt* the sound and spirit of the place: the sound and the spirit was *exactly* Pet Sounds. Also, I let one of the water jets blast into my dick until I jizzed all in the Jacuzzi.
29. Jacuzzi I mean Fugazi
30. A Tribe Called Quest
31. The Steve Miller Band — Basically a solo project, but I'm focusing more on the Boz Scaggs "Overdrive" & Paul McCartney "My Dark Hour" collabo era in me liversnap moind.
32. Radiohead — if they keep the way they're going they're going to be the best rock band *ever*. Thankfully they haven't sunk to the level of some of our weaker and more susceptible bands

into the realm of "electronica"—BARF. A typical British band pratfall. Super-looking forward to *Kid A*.

33. Parliament-Funkadelic
    a. I can't even list all the permutations of this band. Let's just say that they're all good and I like them. I don't know. Though there's no reason to challenge a man wearing a cowboy hat, shag chaps, boom-box pressed to his ears while waterskiing on two dolphins. Everything he does or ever do will flip your wig, doctor.
34. ~~Bandway~~ Public Image Ltd
35. Bandway
36. King Crimson
37. Heart — It pains me to write this, but I think the dudes in the band were just as important as the ladies. (Remember, it's the dissonance that makes Rock *rock*.) Didn't do too much after the old heave ho until Bernie Taupin appeared like a fine, DX7-suffused Scotch mist.
38. Brownsville Station
39. Run-DMC
    a. DMC
    b. Run
40. Mudhoney
41. ~~Ween Supergrass~~ Ween
42. ~~Supergrass Ween Ween Superween Weenergrass Grasserween~~ Supergrass
43. Handsome Boy Modeling School
44. Simon & Garfunkel
    a. Simon
    b. Garfunkel
    c. &
45. Longmont Potion Castle
46. ~~Incubus~~ ~~System of a Down~~ ~~Incubus~~ ~~Incubus~~ ~~Pearl Jam~~ Incubus

47. Grand Buffet
    a. Grape-a-Don
    b. Lord Grunge
    c. Mr. Pennsylvania
48. Babybird / The Yardbirds (tie, weirdly enough.)
49. ~~Mötley Crüe~~ The Smiths
50. The Go-Go's
51. Pantera
52. Queen — No deep cuts!!! WTF!!! Jesus, only at 52, I'm ready for some serious Cheetos action. Need to take a break. This is taking freaking forever.
53. The Breeders — not a bad song between them.
54. Crack the Sky
55. L7 — When we pretend that we're deeaaaaddddddd
56. Boston — Essentially a studio project power duo of Tom Scholz and Brad Delp, but oh what a consonant dissonance they do, this duo does.
57. Aerosmith — The *second best* band from Boston. Well, there's the Pixies too. I don't know. It's all farklempt. Oh, and the Mighty Mighty Bosstones. Shite. ???? !!!! $$$$ &&&& %%%%
58. ~~Butthole Surfers~~ Primus — I can't listen to this band. They are unlistenable with their weird-for-weird's-sake sea-cheese, but by the criteria of my LIST TECHNIQUE™, I must include. The dissonance of these dingles is so dissonary to the max.
59. Kraftwerk
60. Morphine — Boston band better than Aerosmith? Prolly. This whole thing's arbitrary. Like grading poetry. Like dancing about architecture. Like architecting about dancers.
61. ~~Mike + The Mechanics~~ The Cars
    ~~a. Mike~~
    ~~b. The Mechanics~~

62. Polvo
63. ~~Extreme~~
    a. ~~Nuno Bettencourt~~
    b. ~~Gary Cherone —~~ NO you know what. I got a better Boston band. Or Worcester, Massachusetts anyway. J. Geils Band. Talk about dissonance at the heart. The band is named after the guitarist *who wrote zero of the hits.*
64. Strawberry Alarm Clock
65. ABBA — abba abbacadabba… I wanna reach out and grab ya
66. Comus — One of those bands whose first album is a complete artistic statement, like Boston's *Boston* or Van Halen's *Van Halen* or Quix*o*tic's *Night for Day.* Ah, what could have been… Damn you, 1971 United Kingdom Postal Worker's Strike!
67. N.W.A.
    a. Ice Cube
    b. Eazy-E
    c. DJ Yella
    d. Jesse Jaymes
    e. Dr. Dre
    f. MC Ren
68. ~~Trans Am~~ Timbaland & Magoo
69. Boredoms
70. Foreigner
71. ~~Top Down Something something what are they? Bottom Sideways Vagina metaphor thingie JEEZ how hard did you hit that Schwagadelica boy?? oh yeah…~~ Vertical Horizon
72. Boyz II Men
73. Toto
74. ~~In~~ Living ~~Color~~ Colour
75. Color Me Badd
76. Coloured Balls — Sharpie stone *jammers.*

77. The Clash — Gotta have The Clash on here or your list looks like a right twat, innit, guvna?
78. G. Love & Special Sauce — 'stick it in the fridge': the most sexual lyric written in the last hundred years. Band would be at least Top 50 if they hadn't green-lighted the embarrassing "I-76." Sorry Philadelphia.
79. Devo
80. Enon
81. ~~SR-71~~ ~~The Olivia Tremor Control~~ no, definitely SR-71 — the better of the two.
82. Neu!
83. ~~The Dead Kennedys~~ The Association — ?
84. TLC
    a. Tionne "T-Boz" Watkins
    b. Lisa "Left Eye" Lopes
    c. Rozonda "Chili" Thomas
    d. Crystal Jones
    ~~e. David Bowie~~
85. Muzza Chunka
86. Van Halen
    a. Van Halen
    b. Van Hagar
    c. Van Other Singer, that Chick? Oh yeah: Van Scandal
    d. Some other person
    e. All the David Lee Roth reunions and whatnot: Van Union
    f. Vans sneakers
    g. Abraham van Helsing
    h. Get in the Van
    i. Van de Kamp's Crunchy Fish Sticks 100% real fish
    j. Van Phish
        i. Trey Amberstashio (sp?)
            1. Extended JAMS
                a. five man acoustical Jam

b. Jamaican me crazy

2. Phish Food, well actually, okay, hold on…

    a. Ben & Jerry's Top 20 Flavors *RANKED*

        i. Berried Treasure
        ii. Chubby Hubby
        iii. Chocolate Woman
        iv. Mud Pie
        v. Neapolitan Dynamite
        vi. Flavor Flav
        vii. Phish Food
        viii. Triple Caramel Chunk
        ix. Vanilla Fudge Chip
        x. Black Raspberry
        xi. Montlemonpeelier
        xii. ~~Cheesecake Factory~~ Beef Queef
        xiii. Vermontopof-oldsmokey
        xiv. Green Mountain Sweat Gland
        xv. Ethan Allen Furniture Flavor
        xvi. Cherry Garcia

            1. The first chick I ever banged turned out to be a secret hippie. We met at a Memorial Day party the summer before college and did the deed. It was chill, pretty sweet. My manhood was just coming online and I thought handing this girl my V Card might have wings in the

relationship department. But about two weeks later she left to go follow the Grateful Dead. It was totally out of left field. Just a quick phone call and she was gone-zo. Needless to say, I was very confused and very sad. Why had life done this to me? Why had life dangled the proverbial carrot only to hit me in the balls with the proverbial stick instead when I jumped up to lick that tasty icicle-shaped morsel full of healthy beta-Carotene? There were no easy answers. Naturally, I did what any man-child would do: I blamed the Grateful Dead—stupid, old boring noodlers singing siren songs full of noodles. I've moderated my feelings a bit since then, maybe 3%, but at the time I believed in my heart of hearts that what they do is absolutely, 100% *not* what Rock & Roll was meant to be. I'm all for the expansion of borders and the comingling of genres to strange and interesting results, but… Their brand of music was complete shit from beyond the pale, so it wasn't hard to hate them for taking my lady away. Which I soon took as a further insult: *abandoned for a beyond-the-pale-shit band.* I was listening to punk at that time in my life so I doubled down. Black Flag, Minor Threat, Dead Kennedys, The Stooges, Op Ivy, Misfits, et al. In the end though going punk didn't really make me feel any better—just a lot of huffing and puffing—so my friends tried to help the best way they could. Zima after Zima appeared in my tear-soaked hands as if by teleportation that social season. Then, Jägermeister. Healthy, revivifying, I savored the joys of this herbal digestif. As great as this liquid healer was though, I was inconsolable. Raw emotion bubbled up through the viscid, oily, herbal coating of booze like sappy bubbles. At another party on a cold spring weekend some days later I "borrowed" this family's bear skin rug—pulled it right off the goddamned wall—wrapped myself in it and headed for the woods with a bottle of the green stuff. 48-hours later the search party found me, ensconced in my furry rug like a rotten piece of meat in an old taco shell, between a bunch of ferns by a stream in the woods. There were wolves circling me that had to be chased off and the police officer in charge needed to be convinced I wasn't, in fact, a dead bear. I wasn't that though, a dead bear; I was me. And when they unwrapped me from my taco shell, I stepped forth like a god reborn, healed of my pain, steeled against what may come, ready to unleash my soiled, hairy meat unto the earth… *The End.* It's the quintessential Jason Fields story, really—and right at the beginning of my adulthood: Sex, booze, music, the woods: all rolled into one amazing Bildungsroman for your voyeuristic reading pleasure.

xvii. Killington Yard Sale
xviii. Champlain Champagne
xix. Chunky Monkey
xx. Vanilla

3. Lemonwheel HettyBrah
   a. lemons: could I eat a big plate of lemons right now??
      i. YES
      ii. no

ii. Fish Man Drummer
iii. The other guy; bassist
   1. The one who looks like the 3rd Ween brother: Shemp Ween.
iv. The otherer guy—piano man on piano.

k. Van Morrison
l. The Vandals Halen

   m. The band who shot Liberty Van Halence
   n. van hall who am I what is van all this about van? Why? Why? Why? CHEETOZ!!!!!ME!!!!!!!!
   o. Van Veen
   p. and finally: Back to Vanhealin'

87. Tear Da Club Up Thugs
88. Genesis — Two different eras here. '70s Prog Rock maestros vs. '80s Pop Impresarios. Tough. It's a toughie. But I'm going to go with the Peter the Lead Singer version. But if you're talking solo, careers (which I'm not—*don't even*) I suppose Phil's would be higher ranked…
    a. Peter Gabriel
    b. Phil Collins
89. Question Mark and the Mysterians
90. The Velvet Underground — Cool band *RUINED* by Lou Reed.
91. Dandelion — "Weird Out" is my life. Every other song of theirs smokes hot dong. Bong L. McDong. You magnificent son of a bitch. I don't know, I guess "Under My Skin" is good too. Wish it were half the speed. Some bands feel the requirement to do up-tempo songs and it doesn't suit them. They are trying to achieve this level of high-energy Rock & Roll that hardcore punk does so well, but usually leaves the room standing around feeling bad that they can't rise to the occasion of the music, when in reality it's the music's fault. I just want to sink into the grungy sludge of Weird Out for a million years and come out a bog monster that slays all who would defy me. My monster name would be Bong L. McDong and that would be that.
92. Buffalo ~~Dong~~ ~~Tong~~ Tom
93. The Chicago Bears Shufflin' Crew

94. The Wildcats Football Team at the end of the movie Wildcats during the credits, Goldie Hawn, Woody Harrelson and Wesley Snipes, etc. Know what? Fuck it. Let's do this:
    a. Woody Harrelson
    b. Goldie Hawn
    c. The big beatboxing dude.
    d. This other guy… ugh.
    e. Wesley Sniper
    f. Screw it. Too many. Too much VCR rewinding. A+++ song though. Would listen to again.
95. Pearl Jam
96. Roads to Space Travel
97. 311
98. Fleetwood Mac
    a. Stevie Nicks, obviously
    b. et al.
99. The Rolling Stones
100. The Rembrandts

CHAPTER THIRTEEN
Lieutenant Colonel Wildness: Gonezo Insta-Commando

I am trying not to get the shirt dirty. *That's the most important thing to think about*, I think to myself as I step through the tree line at the back of the fairgrounds. The pants I can get muck on. They're black, pre-stressed cargos with cool rips and shreds here and there, as if they were attacked by a pack of wild raccoons at the garment factory. They look better with a little grime on them. You don't want to seem like you just slipped your leggy-weggy pantaloons out of a Sears shopping bag like you're Zack fucking Morris.

But the shirt is something else. And if it's anything, it's an honor.

To be wearing it, I mean.

I walk a hundred and fifty yards into the woods. It is darker and more humid here in the old growth away from the manicured lawn and pretend-forest past the portapotties where teens toke and finger-poke each other, which, as a mental image, alights my passions. Unconsciously I begin making clicking noises. The moon peeks through and my shirt glows in the light. The thing is freaking beautiful—a silky, gorgeous garment spun from the upper lip-hair of angels. I will do my best to describe it, because anything less would be a disservice and insult to the unknown artisans who made it. The shirt I wear—verily, that bodice which adorns my body—is a neon yellow and red bowling button-up short-sleeve shirt with Asian dragons twirling up the back and along the lapels and collar, which are retro and huge. When Nick Hexum pulled it out of a trunk in his trailer and held it up for me to put on I involuntarily held my breath.

Like Pee-wee Herman gazing at his bike I pause there in the dark woods to admire the shirt, smiling down at it. "Good morning… I'm hee-errre," I Pee-wee to myself. I feel like I won the gold in Lillehammer for some winter sport. Maybe all of them. But definitely bob sledding at least.

But what am I doing? Why am I back in the woods? I should be practicing with my new band, slithering my digits up and down the fat, wound metal strings of a sick Fiver for the Fair tomorrow—but for some reason they seemed to want to sleep. "But it's only four in the morning," I said.

"Man, you *are* wild," SA replied.

"Oh, guess I'm just nocturnal."

"The cool thing about being nocturnal is that *all* of your emissions are nocturnal emissions," Chad the drummer (why are all drummers named Chad?) said.

Everyone laughed—maybe me the most—and I left the trailer area for the woods: high-fived Chad for his sick quip, threaded the tech nerds and roadies, waved to that hippie woman Tina in the medical tent and stepped through the trees, feeling the cool hands of destiny massaging me in my fresh duds.

I am drawn to the woods. I am drawn to the woods for answers, even though that's probably not what I am thinking. Needs are questions, I suppose.

It's obviously about Starla. But it's something more. I can feel that. It's a vague sense of belonging mixed with wanting to get to the inevitability of things, but I can't get my head straight nor wrapped around my thoughts. Straight or bent.

Just want to make sure Starla is gone, I tell myself. Just want to make sure she's skedaddled and *that* part of the "Wild Life of Jason Fields" has come to a close. Closed door. Closed book. Closed pants. The look she gave me certainly said it—said she was gone, said 'bye-bye-bye' as the forest exploded with Lilith's light. Did she know the human world was calling me back?

And as I traipse the copses and boscages I am torn. Sweet Starla, you brought me here. You sensed the danger in the woods and you sensed the need of a bass player—you didn't say as much, but you did. I know it. I was chasing you in my silly rage but I was really following you. You lead me here.

And then I see that the woods are empty. No smell, no hoots. My sasquatch has flown her coop.

"Adieu, Starla," I say to the stands of trees shrouded in fog, "Wherever you are, then. Good. Go. Go be with your people. Find your rescue ship and get off this stupid planet. I will stay and represent our wildness, the hairy love we have cultivated. Probably bone a few groupies, yeah, but that's just me. Gotta be me. And same with you. You know that that's not me anymore, Mr. Possessive. Follow your heart, baby. Find some big King Kong daddy and knock out some little space 'squatches. Fly butterfly, fly away, I am setting you free. Go my lady, go, go my lady, you were my butterfly, you have been my sugar baby…"

A teardrop drops down my cheek, illuminated poetically by a tender beam of moonlight. Sadness. Aloneness. I closet that chapter in my life and turn back towards the band—towards the new me, Lieutenant Colonel Wildness… ready for duty.

Which isn't so bad, really. "Not a bad turn of events, really," I say.

And now my brain is filled with thoughts of my new life. They just gurgle up like Old Faithful. Music, parties, celebrity. A boy with a golden bass guitar. Did I have what it takes to hang with these high-powered dudes? I hope I have the chops, I think to myself, stopping to think it. And again the dragon bowling shirt glows.

"I could observe from a distance of ten kilometers your upper-torso apparel, my lover," a giant hairy boulder says, stepping from behind a giant rocky boulder.

"Starla!"

I leap into her arms, blubbering. My furry yurt. She smothers me with kisses, presses me into her layered mats of fur.

Whoa-oh… Was I really ready to give this up?

The shirt is the first thing off. Starla's claws shred it from my body in one motion. It's that old rage of hers, the rage that foments at the sight of clothing—and my body sings with lust. My chest glistens in the moonlight. Then, the cargos—shredded. Gonezo. Insta-Commando.

And instantly, I do not care one lick for a stitch of those prisoner's clothes. I forget all about them…

It's true what they say. Distance makes the heart grow fonder. And the dong grow longer.

We do not speak any further. We get right to it.

Chapter Fourteen
The Horripilation and the Horror

Starla squats low in order that I may reach her dripping sasquatch snatch, her snatchsquatch, like an unfurled sweet, woodsy meat taco dripping with barbecue sauce on a bed of wet ferns. I insert my fingers between her lips and Starla growls. I look up at her in the moonlight and growl back.

My dick stands at attention.

"This cock is a rock," Starla says and takes it in her paws.

Starla wraps her fingers around my veiny shaft and strokes it up and down, up and down. And her magical knuckle-fur caresses me in rainbow patterns fanning out from the main vein. "You are my plaything," she says.

And before I know it, five steps ahead of our usual sex-play, she does her patented maneuver…

Like a mechanical Bat Cave, a black and dripping maw falls onto my face in a mathematically pure arc—sucks me up into itself to swallow me down.

The suction is powerful. A vortex. I am instantly locked in. My feet dangle from my naked body above the dirt.

Starla sucks my head like a lollipop. I feel her saliva

drip down over my whole body, coating me like a cocoon.

My head is all the way inside Starla's mouth. Wet, hot. It's dangerous, this I know. Her teeth are razor sharp. If she doesn't curl her luscious lips over her teeth they would dig into my scalp, possibly decapitate me. Do you like your head? I like my head. Especially where it is. So I let it happen and I don't fight it. I submit to her wants. I let Starla give head to my head. Give my head head. Head my head.

I luxuriate in the weirdness.

Erectify to it.

Weirdness: The essence of my tumescence.

Weird me out.

But then there is that big protuberance thing again. Inside her mouth, it's right in my face. Fleshy yet hard, it's like the soft head of a hard dick.

"Mmf. I— I— cn't… brthe…" I manage to say.

"Take it," Starla says.

"Mmrf?"

"Pet," she says again, and the bulbous thing swings forward and bangs me in the face.

Something in me snaps.

With a strength I didn't know I had—part anger, part exasperation, part Mesozoic-Jurassic fear—I spin my body, un-suction myself from her maw's gummy grip and fall to the leaves.

Starla looks down at me, wide-eyed.

I rise to meet her monkey's gaze. I rise, taller than I seem. I rise strong, powerful, guided by a new light.

The hairs all over my body bristle; goosebumps gone wild. My glowing eyes rise to hers. Is she cowering before my strength? It is my newfound rage, this I know—but bottled. I can control it. I am a bass player.

"I will take you, now, sex bitch," I command.

I want what I want when I want it and I want it now.

"What is—?"

I grab Starla's arm brusquely and spin her body. Her startled surprise is the last look on her face I see as I spin her around like a Spin Doctor and take her mighty haunches from behind.

"*Real* animals…" I seethe.

This is the way real animals do it.

"Y-y-yes…?" Starla mewls.

"Affirmative, female unit," I seethe. Can't fight the seether.

My cock hardens to steel, longer and harder than I've ever seen it. Impressive. I drop it between Starla's two round cheeks, as if placing a weapon on a table, unsettling the complacent dinner atmosphere. Starla groans, circles her hips in anticipation. Lifts her ass like a good girl.

I sneer and grab hold of her moose caboose.

She wants it bad. After weeks of taking the initiative, she wants it this way so very bad—to submit to my pure masculinity. My otherness. My raw power. The deep, dark, devious bass player in my soul.

Starla's musky scent mists upwards. I breathe it in fully: ancient chlorophyll, low-tide-mud, the smoldering reek of a chivvied mastodon. She is ready for my steel.

I slide the head of my cock onto her slippery hole. Rub it up all around in circles. The motion provokes quivers up and down her ass. I see the hair on her back stand, as if spectators at a show.

"Oooooh, p—"

I don't let her finish, no…

I slam my cock deep inside her sasquatch pussy. My hips slam into her bulbous haunches and she screams with surprise.

Harder than a Mack Truck, my dick pounds against her inner wall. Then I drag it out slow, gripping her hips, slow, so slow… Only to pound it in again.

Now I really pound her. And pound her—slide the steel into her softness over and over. Starla's body shakes. She grips the boulder to keep from falling over on her face. Her screams of ecstasy echo throughout the woods, grown silent now to witness our calisthenics. I grab hold of her slender waist and sink my dick deep into her, filling her animal crevasse with my burly hiker.

"Open yourself to me," I command.

Starla's hairy hole, so tight, so hot and wet, gripping my dick, squeezing it… magically opens for me, as if by *Open Sesame*. It pulsates open. And I force my way deeper inside her mysterious caverns

Her voice goes high, stuttering… "Oh, oh, y— y— g— m—…" and trails off in a burble of her alien monster tongue.

And now something else happens…

With each massive thrust, Starla's body moves up the sloping side of the boulder. She grips the stone tight, but I overpower her. And with each massive cock-thrust, inch by inch she moves upward from the indomitable force of my cock-meat until we are fucking doggy-style on top of this massive glacial deposit, fifteen feet around, fifteen feet off the ground.

A moonbeam through the trees illuminates us like a spotlight. I sex up Starla good—my wayward Titaness from the wilderness of the universe—and discover new lands inside her. I split the skins like Columbus sailing into the new world. I take what is new and make it mine.

It was mine all along.

Starla hangs over the side of the boulder now and I grip her bouncing ass and plunge my monstrous girth into her.

She is *all* ass, as far as I can tell. Two massive bags of jello jiggling in the moonlight. That's all I see. That's all I want. I remove a hand from a glute and slide a finger into her little asshole, this tiny doorway on the side of a mountain of hairy flesh. She moans and bucks like a bucking bronco and it's all I can do to keep her from flying off the boulder.

We are like two lovers in a dinghy beset by a hurricane—the boulder our valiant dinghy. To fall off would be the end of us.

"Fuck me, Jason," she coos, "Fuck me harder."

I comply so good. I work her two holes at once: slide a finger in, stretching her tight little ass wider, with two fingers now, and stroke my manhood deep into her, all the way up into her throat.

"Boo ya!"

I laugh and grunt and howl. Heat goes up my spine. I look down at my body and the muscles ripple in the moonlight. They flex and get bigger. This could be confusing to me—why are they bigger? Longer?—but I take it in stride. In my ecstasy I am hallucinating, perhaps, but am I getting hairy now too? A mystical rug of hair pulsates from my skin in tune with my pulsating dick, my balls, the tube of taint connecting the two, as if, like a tube of toothpaste full of hair, extrudes luscious locks of ethereal wool from my pores all over my body.

The truth is plain to me now: I am a Fuck Monster. The horripilation and the horror.

I tilt my head backward and bray to the moon. I pull my finger from Starla's asshole, grip her hips, and begin fucking her with a renewed strength and vigor, like a throbbing jackhammer on steroids. Verily, my tool pummels her pussy.

"Or— or—" Starla stutters.

Our stone dinghy shakes in the forest. Back and forth, back and forth, in time with my in-and-out into her mountain ranges of fur.

"Or what?" I am close to coming. As my pleasure draws strength unto itself and surges like an ocean, my body feels like a piece of macaroni art pulled down from the fridge and shaken apart by the family dog, raging for no reason than because life rewards the rabid.

"Or—"

Now I am the dinghy.

"Or what?"

I am the stone. The hairy house ensconcing my stone-hard wood shakes like an earthquake. Her back straightens. Her muscles go rigid. I would have heard her toes curling and cracking from outer space.

"Or… gasm!" Starla screams, bouncing up and down.

And I fall apart. A white whale of pleasure breaks the surface. Shatters my dinghy of sanity. Majestic and holy. I blast my hot load deep inside her and it shoots out the sides, all over her hairy body, her back and her bum, coating her thick mats of fur with my cum.

Panting… hot… sweaty, lungs begging for air… our respective follicles receding, receding, and riding the waves of diminishing pleasure, the normal sounds of crickets and cicadas picking up through the forest once again, we fall back onto the boulder.

"Oh, my…" Starla moans.

There are those moments in life when you reconnect with an old friend, catch up, and with emotional gravitas make promises of staying closer. It's like a new beginning, when in reality, it was like the last hurrah in a long, slow decline. It's not a hello, it's a good-bye.

If I had known it would be our last time, there on that silly dinghy flying through space, I might have savored the madness a little more.

CHAPTER FIFTEEN
Gymnastic Poetry Juxtaposed Against Discordant, Repetitive Motifs With Insistent Rhythmic Patterns

Starla purrs like a lion and runs her fingers over my hard-edged pectorals, the creases of my six-pack—beechwood aged, tapped in the Rockies, more taste, less filling, wasssaaaaaaaap. "That series of actions was intensely sinkable into my memory banks," she purrs (lion-like).

"Yeah," I respond, my mind up in the leaves. I am normal size now. For what it's worth, during a coitus as all-consuming as that, I felt as if I were ten feet tall. Like a demon had possessed me. There on our stone bed, my body still bristles with the carnal effort, my pores raw and pulsing.

"What, darling pet, came over you?" Starla's voice curls catlike around her words. We're enveloped in the scented fog of our lovemaking.

"I dunno. Maybe the day off, apart—*not* boning. Maybe the band."

"A band?" Starla says, quizzically, nuzzling her muzzle into my armpit. "A band of what?"

It's been such a strange, unbelievable few hours. The blasting light, the hippie healer, P-Nut, the tryout, the shirt selection. I fill her in on the whole story, Behind-the-Music-style.

"Can you believe it? 311!" I say a few minutes later, "They're, like, in my top favorite bands of all time, yo."

"Music is the soul of the universe," Starla says. She's running her hands up and down my satiated body, like stoking embers for another fire. "It heals and purifies and communicates."

"That's exactly how I feel. The dudes in the band feel the same way too."

"What genus of music is it? On my planet, style and substance was codified into a unified system thousands of years ago. I am aware that genre is a subtle and provocative topic on this planet still."

"It's like… *different.* I dunno. Hard to explain. I guess, alternative? But hip-hop tinged? Rapping with hardcore hard rock metal riffs."

Starla sits bolt upright next to me. "Wait!? That was you? That sound I heard through the trees was you? Oh no. Oh no, no, no! I was afraid of this. It is truly happening. We must get away. I thought it was the sounds of a mass transit mishap and collision activating a warning in my hearing systems. We shall go now."

"Whoa, whoa, whoa-oh! There's no way I'm *not* doing this," I say.

"What do you mean by the utterance, do?"

"Do the band. They asked me to join. I'm going on tour with them. I'm on bass, Starla. Can you believe my luck? We're doing Lilith, then Japan, Australia. All sorts of strange and new venues I hear. Outside the box stuff, like Applebutter Festivals. This huge monster truck rally thing. Or what the dudes've told me, anyway. Working different markets, you know?"

"It is imperative that we escape this doomed and unpulchritudinous planet. Instantaneously."

"*Come on*, Star. I mean, stop pulling my leg. Kay? We've been running around like chickens with our heads cut off on this wild goose chase of yours. I mean, it's not going to happen, is it?"

"It *is*."

"When are you gonna tell me the truth of what's really going on?"

"I *did*."

"Oh yeah? Then how is it that we're only five miles from where we started? Baltimore is like, *right there*. You don't even know where you're going do you?"

"Yes, I do."

"Where then? How?"

"The destination is to my planet, for good or worse, come what may. *How*… That is something of which I do not possess the knowledge."

"Arghh!"

"What?"

"Why can't you just be true to me for two seconds!? We just made love so hard that Jesus wept and you can't open up to me."

"I want to. I want to open up to you. However, you will not permit it."

"What? How? I don't get what the hell is the matter with you. You want me to 'be me' for you so you can have me but you want me to do things I wouldn't do unless I was one of you. Starla, I'm so confused and I'm starting to get angry. I don't know what the fuck is going on anymore—if I ever did. It's like, *not* me. I'm a chill party boy. *That's* me. Not this *stressball* you see before you."

"It is highly important to my people that you are you," she says.

"Wait, what?"

"I have seen it happen time and again throughout history, Jason."

"It?" I'm really angry now, my voice hard-edged.

"On many planets. It is the Millennium Virus."

"The Mill—What do you mean?"

"Our sensors have scanned this planet. Cataloged it. It has been on file for centuries. It is known. It is simple science to parse when a world is doomed. Yours is now. That is why I am here."

"You're here to save it?"

"No."

"No—what? You're here to destroy us then?"

"Negative, lover unit. I fear that if I tell you than we will not be able to leave—to uncover the rendezvous."

I shake my head. I'm frustrated. Getting nowhere. "Okay! *Don't* tell me. How? How, then? How is this planet going to explode, like you say?"

"A computer virus."

"That old chestnut."

"Look, Starla. If you want to save Earth, it'll have to be through the healing magic of music—the soul of the universe, like you say, like we did, like I felt in the tree. And I'm about to join one of the greatest healing bands in the world right now. If you wanna be my lover, you gotta get with my friends."

"There is nothing on this planet that can save this planet, love. This planet is doomed. Do you want to die?"

"Better to burn up than fade away."

"What does this response mean?"

"It means… It means I was *born to rock*, Starla. Can't you just be happy for me?"

"Of course I am happy for you. Your happiness is my happiness. But do you not see that happiness is of moot consequence when all of existence will be extinguished very soon?"

"Can't you just go and find the rendezvous point and come back and get me?"

"That is not how it works."

"What do you mean?"

"There is such little time left, Jason. Such an infinitesimal amount of minutes, hours and days left. My internal timing mechanism senses nine days. Nine days approaching. And at the rate we are going, I do not know if we can unlock the rendezvous. There are only nine days left before this blue, habitable planet recombines with the dust of stars."

"Why?"

"As a tree grows from an acorn, the destruction of a planet is inevitable once it has birthed. When the calendar year turns from two-digit-cataloging to four in the time of computer advancement and a society does not take the proper precautions, there is no stopping the collapse."

I burst out laughing.

"You mean the Y2K virus!?" I laugh. I stand and shout. "Gimmie a break! Break me of a piece of that Kit-Kat Bar!!!"

"It is true," Starla says sometime later when I stop yelling and calm down long enough to listen again.

"Call President Clinton then," I say.

"It is much too late for that. The virus is too

insidious."

I shake my head. It's already the year 2000 A.D. The millennium had come and gone, all that misguided Millenarianism, Busta Rhymes' fearmongering nonsense. The Millennium Dome was a big hit. Fireworks, kisses and candy had been given out. We'd made it safely into the future. Nothing had happened—no computer meltdown, no skin of the Earth rupturing with demons and death. Whatever calendar program patch Peter Gibbons was working on in *Office Space* had done the trick. "You may be right," I say and snort. "Clinton's probably too busy getting freaky-deaky with the interns."

"Jason, please communicate to me you understand the calendrical system of this planet's orbit around the sun are ordinal and the new millennium will start with 2001, that there was no year 0?"

"Okay."

"This planet is a prison, Jason. I must convey to you that this world is equivalent to a maximum-security prison. Escape from its gravity field is *very* rare. But we have advance headway on our pursuers."

"A prison? Tell me about it. I used to listen to Tool in high school. 'Why can't we not be sober' and all that," I laugh, I smile, I bounce my eyebrows.

Starla ignores my non sequitur. "...And when the artistic genres of gymnastic poetry are juxtaposed against discordant, repetitive motifs with insistent rhythmic patterns, it is like signing the death warrant of a society. This dissonant music is not a cause of the decline, merely a symptom, but the existence of the symptom is a conclusive indication of imminent destruction. From there, all music will take on the quality of malfunctioning computers. This is not an accident or a 'creative leap,' as it will appear to the progenitors. This is a very real, very dangerous development."

"Look, Starla. I know you think you missed the train to Mars, and you're out here counting stars and shit, but maybe you're wrong. Did you ever think about that? Think about me?"

"I am thinking about you. That is all my brain comprehends and cogitates upon, Jason."

"Then if you really knew me, you'd know I'm wild and this is what I was born to do—to rock."

Starla sits Indian-style on the boulder. "If it is true that you are in possession of greater-than-average 'wildness,' as you say," she says, "why then will not you engage my uvula sexually?"

"Your what?"

"Uvula."

"What's a 'you-view-la?'"

"You are aware, no doubt, of the fleshy protuberance suspended from the top of one's mouth? Just above the throat. Our species do not deviate in this respect. It is common of all auditory sentient beings."

"Oh, *that.* I thought it was your voice box, or something. Your vocal chords, I mean."

"No. It is a uvula. Nestled between tonsils. It is one of the most erogenous places of my species. It terms of love zones, it is the pajamas of the cat, as you are fond of expressing, Jay Jason."

"Oh, right. That thing." A shiver goes down my spine.

"Affirmative."

"I don't know. I didn't realize it was that important. Kinda like sucking a D, though, isn't it? I mean, I'm already inside your freaking mouth. Isn't that enough?"

"Whatsoever most pleases you in the art of lovemaking."

"Starla—look. Starla. I'm not leaving you. I'm not. I don't want to. Why don't you follow me? Follow the band, I mean? Come with us. All across the land. And if we hit up this elusive rendezvous of yours, then we'll take it from there."

"And how would I effectuate this? Without attracting unwanted attention?"

"Maybe you can be a roadie? Those dudes I saw over at the venue are really big. I bet you could fit in with them."

"How many of them are covered head-to-toe in fur?"

"Maybe you can shave it?" I venture. "It's a shame it's not 1992 anymore. Damn, you couldn't tell a longhaired grunger in flannel from a wet pile of hairpieces back then."

Starla stifles a sob. "Maybe it is possible to shave off your skin?"

I've never seen her this emotional. Or any kind of emotional, really, unless steely horniness is an emotion? "Sorry. Look, sorry… okay? So how about just stick around in the woods, then. Stay close. I'll do my 311 thing. We'll love it up animal-style in the woods every night. Perfect, right? Tricked out bliss?"

"There is no amount of extraneous time for this stratagem. We have to escape from this planet first, young pet."

"Ugh!"

"We must get to the rendezvous."

"Jesus Christ on jelly toast!"

I stand and walk around in circles on the boulder. I'm

really irate now. All hetted up. And it begins to all seem very insane to me. How is this even a question? I owe it to Starla for getting me here, but I have to take responsibility for myself now. The course is clear. "Look, I'll ask you *one more* time and you can tell me or not. But if I don't get some answers, it's ol' Jason over to Lilith, okay? And then we'll go from there. Come what may. To be honest, though, I don't think you know where you're going. And if what you say is true, I don't want to die in a forest somewhere with a stomach full of squirrels and pinecones blowing my load into a giant ape. I want to die in a blaze of glory slappin' bass-itude in one of the biggest rock bands in America. The world."

"My heart is breaking."

"No. It's not, Starla. I mean, your heart must be *huge*. Or is it, like, you have three hearts? If one goes kaput you got two more?"

"We are all just little people trapped inside big people."

I laugh. Probably picked that up watching daytime TV—Montel, Phil, Geraldo, Oprah—caged in the Lemaire's house for years. "Look, we've been on the run for weeks now. I have no idea. Months? How the hell long has it been? *Where* are we *going?*"

"You know this. To my homeland. To safety. Away from the Lemaire family."

"Where is that?"

"Very far away."

"How are we going to get there?"

"I cannot say."

"WHY! Why can't you tell me?"

"I just cannot, my love. Oh, please, cannot you trust

me? It is not permitted. Have I been anything but honest with you? Do you not see how it pains me that I cannot divulge the means? When I really am not sure as well?"

"Okay. Whatever. Work with me then, would you? How do you *think* we'll get there? Across the universe?"

"Love."

I scream. So very loud. I rise up on my tippy-toes and nearly blow out my uvula screaming into the treetops. My balls ring with ache.

Starla reaches out a monkey paw to me. I recoil from her touch. I try not look at her, but the moonlight glinting off the tears on her dimpled face is unavoidable. For some reason this bugs me, eggs my anger on. *Duplicitous nature, using my urges against me, the soppy tears of a woman, would drown you if they could, drown the whole freaking world*, I think.

"Lover…" Starla whispers.

"No," I say. "If it's like you say and music is the soul and healer of the universe, than this is my chance to become one with the universe. I'm doing it for the both of us. You don't think I know what was going on up in the tree? Our great ode to the stars? If music is so important, than this is our one chance to really sing out joyfully to the Milky Way and shit. This is our one real chance to save the world. This is our one chance to connect with something bigger than us."

That whole thing about it being darkest before the dawn? That's dumb—makes no sense. The sleepy, early-morning earth gets flooded with that obnoxiously pale blue light for like an hour before dawn. It gets brighter and brighter. If you're being levelheaded about darkness, it is so obviously darkest when the sun is antipodal to you on the far side of the earth. Starla and I are very clearly at this point. Antipodal, parallax, whatever. It is so dark we are blind to each other. "Do you not see, Jason?" Starla says, "There is nothing bigger than us."

I jump down off the boulder. What she said stings, and flicks me in a feeling place, but I've already made my decision.

"I don't care if my sasquatch lover says the world is going to explode in nine days," I say. "I'm an artist, and when a band like 311 asks you to play bass for them, you do it. Because it's the new *freaking* millennium. Ugh!"

I turn and head for the Lilith Fair, scooping up swatches of my shredded neon clothes from the forest floor as I go.

"I cannot wait long for you," Starla says after me, whimpering.

"Fine with me!"

"I will wait one day and one night here at this stone for you." I can hear her tears hitting the dry leaves behind me like rain.

"Don't bother!"

"After one cycle of the sun I must leave."

"Great! Go!"

Her crying could drown me out here in the woods. Knock me down like a flooding river before I could have my grand debut.

I make trails for the Lilith Fair.

And to destiny.

CHAPTER SIXTEEN
Equidistant to All Warring Parties

"You're on the website, dude."

The internet? I wasn't into the internet—didn't stroke my boat. Nothing had really impressed me so far as to warrant all the hullaballoo around it: AOL chats with men pretending to be girls talking to other men pretending to be girls like some kind of lathered loathing-vortex. I'd received exacting only one "*e*-Mail" in my life (sent to the e-Mail address given to me by my alma matter, like a mother duck feeds its young) and it was an African prince asking for my bank account numbers. Of course, there were some things I enjoyed, things that tickled my pickle: TheSpark.com was pretty legit: I dug the Stinky Meat Project, the Fat Project, the Burnmaker and their quizzes like the Bitch Test and the Lazy Test and stuff. And all the guitar tabs sites. I wouldn't be sitting in 311's dressing room today if it weren't for those. And there probably wasn't a 'net 'site that I hadn't Mr.T-ified, hanging out in the college computer lab, fucking around on their dedicated dial-ups when I should have been doing homework. I even T'inated one of my Psych papers and my teacher didn't notice. Talk about instant word-count boost! I pity the provost.

So I'm a little confused as to why the band is so jazzed up to show me that I am "on" the 'net. I squint down at the chunky, strawberry-red iMac G3 and look at the pixelated picture of me, depixelating in waves to a minimal JAY-Peg clarity. It was from the previous night. I am on stage, still wearing my colorful hippie groin-scarf, jamming out with the band. Under the picture it reads: "Welcome to our newest member Jason Fields! ;-P you rock!"

"Wow," I say, "Neat."

"Dude's a little less than psyched," SA says.

There is some laughter around the dressing room. Some nervous. Some bordering on *in-a-castle-keep* malevolent.

"No, it's just… No, it's cool," I say, standing upright. I'm wearing a new set of futuristic bowling attire. The band didn't seem to care that I'd stumbled out of the forest naked yet again, or ruined the first outfit. Maybe they think it—nudity—is 'my thing.'

"Yo! Leave the guy alone! He don't like the web, he don't like the web!" lead guitarist Tim Mahoney rails from the couch.

"Eat a donkey, Mahoney," singer Nick Hexum says.

"Takes one to know one," Tim replies, acidic.

"Okaaaaay," Chad the drummer says. "Guy-yyyyyyyys, come on…"

It seems that I've walked into an ongoing dispute, stuck my dangler in a big mangler of it. Far from being the heaven of rock and puss that I thought it'd be, 311 are at each other's throats.

Nice.

I mean, I should have known. Every fiefdom has their own petty squabbles and issues that make no sense outside their borders. A band is like a five-way relationship. Every member has a relationship with every other member. The Hallmark Channel is chock full of tiny violin symphonies and heartstring yankers: the sailor that got away; the divorcée lookin' for love in all the wrong places until the right place bonks her upside the head; the pumpkin spice that turns into a Spice Girl. Now, imagine if it was twenty-five storylines going at once in one made-for-TV movie. Five times five. That's what a band is. And that's what 311 is.

There appear to be two main camps in this Family Feud. Some of the guys want to take the band in a new direction and some are fine with things as they are. (It's that goddamn *Armageddon* vs. *Deep Impact* thing again.) And as I realize what's going on, I keep my mouth shut—don't make any sudden moves or proclamations. I freeze in the center of the room. I don't want to alienate anyone, end up on the outs. Not when I am *so* close to superstardom.

"Come on guys, we're supposed to be chillin'. I love chillin' before a show," Chad said. "We used to chill so hard, listen to chill reggae grooves and get ourselves in the mood. That used to be us. Not *this*." Chad the drummer was definitely on the side of keeping things as they were, hard-edged and hip-hopping, but he also didn't dig all the infighting. He appeared to mediate more than the rest. I guessed it was because he was the drummer and no one in a band respects the drummer (except maybe a percussionist?), so tried to stay equidistant to all warring parties.

There is more squabbling that goes over my head for ten or fifteen minutes.

"Look, Jason. Sorry about all this. You've really

walked into something," Nick says after a bit. He's smiling at me, embarrassed.

"I mean, that's okay, dudes. Sorry you're going through this," I say.

"Mighty magnanimous of you, J-Dawg," SA says.

"I mean, that's why The Killer's got us at Lilith. We're here to expand our fanbase, man," Nick says. "So why not embrace the new, ya know?"

"Who's Killer?" I ask. "*The* Killer?"

"Our new manager. The best. Killer ain't no joke, man. You mess with The Killer, you get the wrong end of the stick, nah'm heard?" Nick says.

"After this we're joining up with a monster truck rally tour. S'gonna be the bomb, yo. Loud as all git out! Hee yaw!!!" SA proclaims.

"Cripes," Tim says.

"Tiiiiiimmmm," Nick says. "Chill."

"Why?" Tim says. "Fuckin' why? Why do we have to open up for giant monster trucks and a crowd of menstrual cases?"

"Much as I hate to say it, y'all, P-Nut was right. We're stagnating, man," Nick says. "We're in a rut, y'all. Like a monster truck spinning its wheels in fifty feet of mud."

Mention of the erstwhile bass player P-Nut perks me up. "Don't wanna rub salt in any wounds," I say, "But what was up? I mean, why'd P-Nut jet?"

"He wanted to take us in a new direction for the new millennium. I just don't think he had any idea how to do it," Nick says. "But *I* do. I do now."

"No," Tim says. "*Dammit.* No."

"P-Nut was the heart and soul of 311, Jason. He was a true artist. I mean, you saw the leg. But like all geniuses…

troubled, ya know?" drummer Chad says. "Never could really express what he really wanted to say except with his tasty licks."

"If we don't evolve, we're dead meat," SA says. "Those lovely ladies out there in Lilith Land are going to eat us alive. We need to bring the dope beats, yo, the hip-hop flavor they *crave*."

I take all this in. The band continues to argue. It gets really heated and I press my back against the wall to avoid the fray. Nick gets in Tim's face, SA gets in Chad's face. They face off six ways till Sunday like in *Slapshot*. "Screw this!" Tim eventually screams and heads for the door.

"Don't let the door hit you where the good Lord split you!" SA yells after him.

"No…" I whimper, to myself mainly, quietly bereft. "Please." They're going to break up before I can heal the universe with my bass magic.

Tim reaches for the door. But Nick steps in front of him. Are they going to duke it out? Eep. I step back.

"Wait," Nick says.

Tim freezes—looks at Nick. We all do.

Then Nick holds up a CD-R. The disc catches the overhead light and flashes in our eyes.

"What the crap is that?" Tim says.

"The future."

"No."

"Hear me out."

"Get *out of my way*, Nick."

"Please… just—"

"Move!"

"Just *listen!*" Nick says.

"To what?"

"*Kid A.*"

There is immediate silence in the room. Everyone stares at Nick. Silence, except for the barely audible, muffled strains emanating though the walls of Lisa Loeb performing on the main stage with very special guest Me'shell Ndegeocello. Finally, Tim speaks again: "Are you kidding me? Are you joking us right now?"

"Nope," Nick says with a lapel-to-lapel grin.

"How…?"

"That's not coming out till October. *Rock*tober," Chad says in reverent tones.

"As it just so happens, The Killer—K Dawg—got us an advance copy. Something about holding up David Fricke by the neck until it fell out of his jeans pocket…"

"Whaaaaa!"

"…the new Radiohead album, y'all! K copped it to me last night. I wanted to surprise you after the show but—fuck it, it can't wait. I can see it can't wait. I scoped it last night, and dudes… It is *too* good. And I think you'll see what I mean when I say it is a shot across the bow of rock music and undeniably the new direction."

No one says a word. We all watch as Nick walks over to the strawberry iMac, opens the CD tray on the front and slips the disc in.

CHAPTER SEVENTEEN
Group Hug, Slowly I Turn

I wander the Fair. It is day. I'm exhausted. All who wander may not be lost, but I am loster than a lobster at a cat show. So much has happened in the last 24 hours it's as if my brain can't take in anymore. No room at the inn. Hit the bricks, visual information.

Everything I see goes in one eye and out the other. There is an ocean of women and women-like men covering the fairgrounds. Fun colors, flower print dresses, taut pig tails, lace chokers. Everything I could ever want and more in an undulating sea of malleable, spreadably-soft-like-Parkay clam, and I take no notice.

There is always something humid about these festivals. Like the sweat glands can't get a breath in edgewise—there's too much sweat and it evaporates off the skin and just *sits there* at eye-level like smoke from a barbecue. Maybe this is an evolutionary thing. A herd needs to slip and slide all over each other to move efficiently. That, or it's the lady juice escaping panties and evaporating into the air. Either way, my bowling attire is drenched. Of this too, I take no notice though. Just slide along through the juicy, slimy herd.

My mind is racing. *Was Starla right?* I think. I couldn't

believe how quickly things had gone the way she said they would…

Nick put the CD in the 24x CR-ROM tray and immediately the computer starts going haywire. Spinning, buzzing, whirring, clanking.

"Eek!" Tim yells.

Chad makes a wounded face and plugs his ears with two drumsticks.

"The CD-R must be corrupted or something," SA shouts over the din, walking up to the strawberry cube on the table. The sound is getting worse. I back up, expecting the iMac to explode any second. "Shitty $1,500 computer with upgraded 512 RAM thingie!" SA shouts over the noise.

Nick steps in front of him, keeps SA from whacking it. "No! You suckas! This is the music."

"Whaaat?"

"This is *Kid A*."

"No fuckin' way."

"I listened to it on my Discman™ last night, yo!"

And sure enough, Thom Yorke's voice slithers from the translucent desktop computer. He's singing something over the digital malfeasance, it's hard to tell what noble sorrow—or what creature, exactly, whether from the woodland or perhaps one of those nasty animals that survive in an urban environment like an opossum or rat, is there with him in the sound booth, attached to his testicles with its beastly claws, stabbing, squeezing, scraping and just all around *abusing* his little man-grapes—is causing him to sing that way.

Fifty minutes later, the CD ends.

Nick stares at his bandmates, smiling, eyebrows

high—nearly meeting the roots of his yellow hairline. “So? Huh? Right?”

“Wow,” SA says. “That’s bananas!”

SA was always onboard with a new, bold direction. Always the gearhead, I guess there were enough slammin’ beats on *Kid A* for him to sign up.

Everyone turns to Tim.

Tim gets up and paces the room. “It’s fucking lasers farting and computers going, Hi, I’m broken, will someone please fix me,” he says, agitated.

“Oh, so you…” SA queries.

“It’s all outtakes from a shitty Aphex Twin album!” Tim shouts. Veins are popping on his forehead. His hands are shaking. He makes for the door.

“So what are you saying, you—”

“I love it!” Tim screams, spinning around.

Nick, SA and Tim hug and pound.

The tide turned, Chad, spineless drummer, has no recourse but to say he likes it and pretend it’s his own choosing. He joins the group hug. It’s unanimous. The critics agree. *Kid A* is a triumph.

And then slowly the group hug turns to me.

Oh right. Me.

I am sweating in the corner, breathing fast and shallow, seeing stars, clutching my bass like a security blanket. *Kid A* has ripped me a new one. A new *Kid A-hole.* Is this the apocalypse? The sound of computers… What had Starla said? Broken computers or something… Creative leaps? Shit. Why was I such a dick to her on the rock? Dicks don’t have ears and never listen.

“Well, whadaya think, Jace?”

“I don’t know, it’s… *okay,*” I exhale, gulping. The

perspiration has soaked through my shirt.

"Okay!?" everyone shouts at once.

"Hey, don't listen to me! I'm just the new guy! I mean, I'm a 311 fan. Of course I like what you were doing in the past! It's just..."

"Got any other *great ideas* for us, then, new guy? Got anything that will get us out of our creative slump?"

I gulp again. It hurts. My throat is dry. Dizzily, I try to think of old styles of music, odd combinations like ska and rhumba, but I got nothing. I'm not sure what to do—don't know who or what to believe anymore. Broken computers and creative leaps... Even if the world is going to explode in nine days, I don't feel like I have the strength for even just one more. I won't even *make it* to the apocalypse. "How about..." I quiver, "What about, uh... Have you guys ever thought about, um, Mr. T-ifying your music?"

Chapter Eighteen
A Bombastic Cavalcade of Music

Somehow I get out of the greenroom still in the band. I make enough hedging comments and gargle enough semisweet adulation towards our British saviors to stay in 311 for at least this one gig.

I walk out of the room, down a hall, and find a door. I open the door and go outside. The sun is uncomfortable, nauseating. I press forward. There are people milling around. I walk through them and after some time make it to a place where there are more people. The people are more crowded here. They all seem to be facing in one direction. They move as one to the sounds coming from a place far away from them. The sound moves them.

And then I realize that I am moving too. Swaying to it. What is this sound?

I start to wiggle from my daze.

A band is playing on a stage. It's another all-dude band. Guess Lilith needed to beef up the roster or something.

I look around to locate where I am in relation to the festival and see that it's one of the side stages, reserved for new acts—undergrounders and up-and-comers. A woman is gyrating next to me in time to the band. I see how the music heals a spiritual wound within her. She is really into it—her swinging pig tails nearly decapitating me like two whizzing nunchuks.

"Who is that? What band is this?" I ask her.

"You don't know?" she says, not stopping her gyrating nunchukery to answer.

"No."

"Nine Days."

"Uh, what!?"

Nine days? This is confusing. And scary and suddenly not cool anymore. Starla was always harping that there were nine days left—that in nine days would be the destruction of the whole kit and caboodle. But when did she say that? It seems like a thousand years ago now, but it was probably only yesterday or the day before. "What did you say?" I ask the pig-tailed chick again.

"They're Nine Days."

"Ohhhh… The band is *called* Nine Days?"

"Yes."

"Weird."

"*You're* weird."

I shake my head and wend my way forward through the crowd, drawn to the healing sound. After the auditory assault I'd just suffered in the greenroom, the earthy, organic rock sounds of this Nine Days band are like a sweet balm to my ears. Guitars, bass, drums, keys, singer—all doing what they're supposed to be doing. There is no horsing around. No pretention. No hard drives grinding. No shredding Zip Disks like parmesan on a cheese grater or lasers in 9/8 time. It's classic, this music—anointed by history. So classic it's like, *new*, what they're doing. It's a breath of fresh air for my clogged glands.

I make it to the front of the ladycrowd. I press myself against the barricade, squeezed from behind by a wall of undulating female meat.

And my troubles just disappear… Classic American Rock, man. This will never go out of style. *This will save the universe*, I think to myself as I bob my head and shake my hips in time to the smooth four-on-the-floor beats and moderate rock tempo. If I had pigtails I'd definitely be swinging them around, for sure.

I look up at the band on stage to find out just who or what is making this joyful noise.

There are five men in Nine Days. I can see why the girls in the audience are going wild for them. All have stylish soul patches, all with smaller chins than the next guy, all small and safe, with slim, suave, non-predatory physical bodies. We're talking cute hair, cute noses and eyes. They're like a band of elves. It's Rock & Roll with capital R's, but none of that scary counter-culture shit, none of that long-haired crypto-, bag-eyed, stoop-shouldered and craven, vagabond-loner '90s stuff. The lead singer is the cutest with his short-cropped brunette coif and soulful baby-blue eyes—I can see and respect that, even without being swayed sexually by it (though I do have a chub of course, mashed against the barricade in front of me and between three and five unseen mystery breasts pressed against my upper-back at all times during this). If these guys don't wind up bigger than the Beatles (#2 on my list of 100 Top Bands of All-Time), there is definitely something askew with the universe.

Then the music ends. "Thank you, Lilith Fair!" the singer sings into the mic. The crowd goes wild. So much cheering. I cover my ears; I smile, but cover my ears.

"Thank you, and good-day to you! We've been Nine Days from Long Island, New York!"

The band start to load up their gear but the crowd is unceasing. They want more. "More! More! More!" they scream. "Encore! Encore! Encore!"

Hearing this, the singer talks to a guy with a clipboard wearing a headset in the wings, and comes back to the mic. "Okay. We got time for one more! Thank you! Thank you!" he shouts, strapping on his guitar, and the ladies go bananas.

What the hell. I even scream too.

Then the band launches into their encore song and I know my life has been changed forever.

It's a doozy.

"This is the story of a girl / who cried a river and drowned the whole world," the singer sings, accompanying himself on guitar with these devastating and angular chord changes. There is so much inherent tension in what is happening in this briefest of intros that I stop breathing. *What will happen next?* it's as if my very being yearns to know. "And though she looks so sad in photographs / I absolutely love her when she smiles…" and the entire band kicks in with a bombastic cavalcade of music that wallops me into thankful, ecstatic submission.

A joke. Instantly I realize all my so-called "wildness" has been a joke. I've been phoning it in. On fumes. 1-800-FUMES-a-LOT. Who am I? Why did I think I needed to join 311 to be myself? All this wildness was nonsense—that's what Nine Days are telling me. This healing, awesome and emotionally powerfully music—that's what it's telling me—it is calling me back to myself. I'm like a No-Limit Soldier, except a Limit Solder. I realize my wildness has limits. I'd reached the end. I am ready to take the next step.

And I know in a heartbeat. I need to be with Starla. It was a mistake to leave her. I imagined her tears drowning me—the entire world—out in the woods when I left her on the boulder and the Nine Days song is letting me know what a fool I was to leave her alone. Whether or not she was telling the truth about all this End of Days stuff, the Lemaires, the rendezvous, the howling at the moon, the squirrels… it doesn't matter. I love her and want to be with her. I'd follow her hairy haunches anywhere. There in the crowd I see her true spirit, the Little Starla in the Big Starla. When you're already a wild-ass wild man of the woods, what would be the wildest thing you could possibly do? Join a rock band? Do wild and squishy things with wild groupies in wild tour busses? No. Absolutely not. The wildest thing you could do is settle down with your big booty momma, your very special lady, treat her right, let her know how amazing she is each and every day of your short life on this Earth. Wildness is forever parallax, antipodal to where you are, no matter what.

I start to cry. The emotional power of this song has fixed me. The healing power of music! Dang! There it is.

Little vignettes—little brainstorms—play in my mind's eye of the recent past. My so very loving life with Starla on the run, on our motorcycle, sexing her body, sprinkling water on her chocolate. I think of the time in the top of the trees, before we were so brutally interrupted by the blinding light of the human world. The tree spun, gliding over all of nature while I licked her hairy pussy, and Starla's riveting orgasm like an elegy to the heavens—her body glowing amber and gold, the true color of her energy visible to me for the first time. And then how our voices, ringing like a bell, twisted like a sonic tube up into the starry skies.

Nothing good comes easily, I think to myself. *Sometimes you gotta fight.*

I didn't know how long Starla was going to wait for me. Suddenly I was in a panic. What if she's already left? Oh no! I spin and turn to the back of the fairgrounds. The woods are so far away—through a thick, viscous crowd of surly women. The sun is setting. It is evening. Oh no! What if I miss her? It can't wait. Screw 311 and fame! I don't need it. I need Starla and nothing else.

I begin to carve my way through the crowd.

But then something is holding me back.

"Holy crap, *there* you are!" a man to my right with a low, gruff voice suddenly says from the other side of the security barricade. He has my arm in a death grip.

"Hey! Wha—?"

"Dude, you're on in *five* damned minutes!" the guy says. He's burly. I recognize him, one of 311's roadies. "We been looking all over for you, little bass boy."

"No… um," I say, "I…"

"No what?" he says, forcefully, uncomprehending. He has small, close-set eyes. Ape-like, in an uncool way.

"I don't want—I don't think—I'm…" I say, withering under this man's grip and gaze. He shakes his head—ain't no time for what this little bass boy is feeling inside in the feeling place—and yanks me back towards the main stage.

Chapter Nineteen

Mmm… Amber Gold Something Something

"What the hell am I supposed to do with this?" I ask.

I don't even know what it is. Some kind of machine. I thought I had a pretty good grasp on the latest music gear and technology. But *this* thing: I have no idea.

It's my first gig with 311. And this is how it's going down…

We're already on stage. And clogged all over it is stuff I've never seen before. It's piled everywhere: banks of synthesizers that look like switchboards from the 1950's, some guy with a violin, a couple others with harps and tubas, the aforementioned strawberry iMac. The only similarity between 311's setup before and after is SA's turntable rig.

How did they get all this new stuff so fast?

"I know it's not what you're used to," Nick says to me. "Don't worry about it. Just let the spirit in the machine move you, dude, okay? You got the skills, so let's go pay the bills with those skills, hey?"

"I mean, I don't know…" I trail off.

"Here, yo. Just do *this*." Nick hovers his hands over

the little gray box he's given me and taps on a keyboard attached to it. This sound that sounds like the sound of two penguins fucking inside an electric generator explodes out over the Lilith Fair. The crowd. I try not to look at the crowd—it's too big, it's amazingly huge—but I can't help but see all the women in the front row cover their ears in pain. *I feel ya, ladies*, I think to myself. "It's infrared," Nick says. "The future. Dig it!"

Before I can question Nick further though, he tucks into the iMac—begins stroking keys and moving the little, strawberry-colored hockey puck mouse around. His face glows in the screen. I see that his microphone is attached to it—probably got a sick sound card. He pulls the mic from the stand and starts singing into it. Nothing happens. No sound comes from the PA. At first, anyway. I guess he was just setting sounds up in Pro Tools or something. Because a few seconds later this horrific, stuttering loop of his voice, like a horse swallowing a whale, digitally, comes screaming across the sky.

The loop doesn't stop. Good Lord, why doesn't it stop?

But rather than tackle Nick, or yank the power cord from his iMac like they should, the rest of the band do exactly what they should *not* do…

They start jamming along with the horrific loop.

Or rather, coat his loop with more execrable computer noise. "Jamming" would denote that they somehow are in time with the loop, or add any kind of melodic or rhythmic dressing whatsoever to what is already there. Even Tim, the guitarist's guitarist of all guitarists, is just sitting there, pounding on an old-school Korg sequencer, twiddling twaddle from the circuits. Chad drums on an upturned kettle drum and rusty triangle. It sounds like an art school noise band.

This is my worst nightmare.

I stand off to the right of the band on the stage, frozen. I just stare at them. I look at the crowd. I wince. I can see how upset and confused everyone is. And then, right on cue, the first boos hit us.

We were lucky as men to even get this gig. They were gracious to let 311 play, and gracious to applaud and cheer when we came out on stage. Now, I'm no Miss Manners, but I think it's in pretty poor taste to just wank off on stage into a bunch of computers like we were wanking our dinks. It's just *not gonna go over well.* The last thing anyone in *this* audience wants, frankly, is our frank 'n beans.

On cue, the crowd gets nasty. Daddy fat nasty. Plastic bottles start raining down on us. I duck out of the way at the last second; a steel-toed boot nearly kills me.

What the hell? I'm not even doing anything! I want to shout at the crowd, but I stop myself. There is an entire row of trapezoidal-jawed, teed-off lesbians at the front that I don't want to fuck with.

"We want 'Down!' We want 'Down!" We want 'Down!" they chant, pounding the barricade—a motif that's actually more musical than what's happening on stage.

Nick steps to another mic. A clean mic. "Sorry, ladies. This is the future. Our new direction. Ya'll'll *get it* eventually."

Soon the entire fairgrounds are screaming bloody murder. "Down! Down! Down!" comes the chant.

"Just pretend you're at the Newport Folk Festival and we're Bob Dylan!" Nick says into the mic. Then, with the click of his mouse, he loops "we're Bob Dylan" over and over again, adding flanger, reverb, ring modulator and squelching the lows and highs in a vicious EQ-knob titty twister.

The entire fairground starts shaking with rage. A light above us shimmies loose from its screws and smashes on the stage into a million shards. I begin to fear for our safety. "Give us the dope beats we crave!" screams one of the lesbians in the front row. And the bottles continue to rain down. It's going to be a fucking bloodbath—Woodstock '99 shit. This is supposed to be the anti-all *that shit* at Lilith, and here we are very much enabling all *that shit.* Because why? Because computers?

Something has to be done.

Tina Turner was right. We don't need another hero, but desperate times call for desperate measures (by heroes). (Thunderdome.)

"Fucking fuck it!" I yell.

I sprint backstage—bust into the greenroom and snag my bass. Before anyone can stop me I run back out on stage and plug it in with a few inadvertent *bzzrt* sounds. The laser-thingie-box I was using was actually feeding through a bass amp, so I'm already set.

At this point, the band cotton on to what I'm doing. Some of them let up on their unyielding sound-collage to gawk at my indiscretion.

It's all the pause I need.

I walk to the center of the stage. The crowd is going apeshit (and believe me, I know ape shit when I see it). The whole wild world is before me, screaming into my face. It is a wall of angry humanity. The jeers actually lift the hair from my head like a hurricane. My lapels flap in the breeze, threaten to launch me like a parachute. I've never been so scared…

Ain't no stopping now. I just go for it.

I play bass.

My fingers do the walking. I don't think. I just noodle. My brain has no capacity for thought. I soak the fairgrounds in my greasy, low-end vibeage. I drench them in my licks like rain on parched earth.

Eventually, my fingers hit on this riff. There's something about. It feels like home. I go with it. It is chill. Smooth. Chill and smooth, yet shrouded in hard-edgery—everything that I thought 311 stood for. It sounds familiar to me, but I'm not sure what it is. I keep playing it.

Little-by-little, the crowd stop jeering, the crowd's levels of imminent riot diminish.

And one-by-one, the band stop their cacophonous frank-wankery to listen.

Where did this riff come from? I think. *Where have I heard it before?* I think, as I keep on keepin' on.

And then it hits me.

P-Nut.

This is P-Nut's riff, the O.G. bassist I replaced.

The first night I came out of the woods and heard 311 sound checking, P-Nut started playing a riff in the middle of two songs. This *very* riff. Then after that… the band fight and everything else. Wow—I really must have been listening with my subconscious and soul. Because I am just nailing it. Nailing it note for note.

And then I am moved to sing. As if just orgasming with a horny Bigfoot at the top of a pine tree, my heart yearns to sing. I got some things I want to sing about. Namely: Starla, my muse, my life.

I walk to the clean mic. "Brainstorm, take me away from the norm…" I sing-speak in time with the riff. Then, something of a verse: "Mmm… amber, gold, something something something. (And then the chorus, I think…) Whoa-oh… Amber is the color of your energy. Whoa-oh… shades of gold, uh, something naturally…"

"Hey man, that's dope!" Tim Mahoney yells. He picks up his guitar and starts riffing along. Straight jamming. He adds this cool little lick as a counterpoint, adding a whole new level of complexity to the nascent hootenanny.

It doesn't take long for the rest of the band to chime in. Nick takes over vox and adds his own flair. Then Chad adds a fresh reggae beat. *What a groove.* Wow, I wasn't even thinking reggae at all. P-Nut must have been, though—heart and soul of the band that he was—because it feels natural and so damn good.

The band needed a new direction and P-Nut knew. P-Nut *knew*, man. Not this futuristic bullshit, not harder and harder music, but a revamping—a re-chilling back to 311's roots as a roots-reggae band.

Nice.

And then I look over and see P-Nut! He's standing just off stage. He is smiling ear to ear. He is nodding his head, totally blissed out. We make eye contact. And rather than be pissed or anything grotty-max 5000 like that, he motions for me to look at the crowd. I look and see that the entire venue is into it. A wave of healing energy spreads out over the crowd, over the front-row lesbians, the thousands behind them and out into the forest and entire world. And then magically the chorus comes around again and the entire Lilith Fair knows it by heart. They sing along. They nail *every word*, just from listening to it once.

"Whoa-oh… amber is the color of your energy… Whoa-oh… shades of gold, uh, something naturally…" sings the entire venue, so loud and with such pure, loving hearts, in fact, that it would be thoroughly impossible for any kind of, say, rescue spaceship passing through the solar system to have any chance whatsoever of missing it.

Now it's my turn to motion. I motion to P-Nut to come out on stage. He does. "The return of Mr. P-Nut!" I yell into the mic and a good-hearted cheer goes up.

My next move is as natural as the sun and moon moving across the sky…

I slip off the bass and hand it to P-Nut. He takes it with a noble, eyes-closed bow of the head and I make a "We're Not Worthy" bow to him.

There is nothing left for me to do but to abscond with my bad self.

I walk backwards off the stage, hands raised, the crowd screaming. I look over at Nick and he mouths "Thank you" towards me, smiling that devilish, rock god grin of his. "Thank you."

I nod my head to this new "Amber"-hued song, truly made of star stuff, and head towards the backstage area.

And to destiny.

Chapter Twenty
Nine Days Wild

Sweet release! How many times have I tasted freedom on this journey? Every new freedom tastes better than the last. It is a flavor that does not diminish. Sometimes our old desires come to us later in life when we don't really need them anymore, like a semi-chub wrapped in laurels. If you're mature, you wipe the chubby away and say, "No thank you, for my desires have changed." As I plan my escape the hell up outta here, I commend my magnanimity and Zen-like powers of, uh, Zen, for seeing how the jig was up for me and my Rock & Roll dreams and how my old dreams were keeping me from the true freedom of now. Bass just wasn't me any more, man.

This is the new me. This is my new plan…

1. Get the hell up outta here
    a. remove bowling attire
    b. wend through
        i. lesbo-thick fair
        ii. nunchuk hair
        iii. glandular air
2. Go to Starla, waiting for me on our dinghy
    a. apologize
    b. "sprinkle water on chocolate"

You'll notice that stopping to thank Nine Days isn't anywhere on this list, but that's what happens. Why not?

I am sprinting through the backstage area, unsheathing my body from my prison clothes. I rocket down one hallway, then another. "How the hell do I get up outta here!?" I shout. I don't stop to hear the answer from anyone who tries to help me. I'm too jazzed up. Spazzed, yup. Then, as if by Fate, I run by Nine Days' dressing room. "Nine Days," I see in a blur on the door as I hurl past.

I stop, hard on my heels.

With tears of gratitude in my eyes, I knock on the door.

I have to thank them. I have to congratulate this band on their accomplishment, of how their song "Absolutely (Story of a Girl)" is the story of my life. I have to let them know how special they are and what they've done for me before I disappear into the woods forever. It would be in poor taste not to let them know how amazing they are and that, quicker than a squirrel shakes its tail, there will be a revamping of my Top 100 Bands of All-Time List.

There is sound coming from behind the door, but no one answers. I put my ear to the door. There is the muffled sound of a TV. Possibly also the sound of engines, cars on TV.

I knock again. Nothing.

Again, there is the sound of a TV. Definitely some kind of loud engine. Then I hear groans. What's going on?

I test the doorknob. The door opens.

"Knock knock," I say, coming into the room, "Hey, what's up, Jason here… 311 bassist? Well, used to be, anyway. But I just wanted to say how much I think you guys kick so much—"

The band is sitting in chairs looking up at a television in the corner of the room. Eyes glued. No one moving. No one acknowledging my presence.

On the TV I see someone I recognize. It's a woman, but I can't place where I know her. She's speaking to a news reporter. She has to yell because somewhere behind her is the sound of incredibly loud engines revving and roaring.

"—an amazing discovery. An amazing scientific discovery and an amazing opportunity for cross-promotional purposes," the woman says.

"Where did you find it?" the reporter asks.

"Where else? In the woods!" the woman laughs a horsey laugh.

I know that laugh, I think.

And before I can think anything else with my dumbass brain, the woman's name appears under her on the screen: Athena "The Killer" Diller, Music and Entertainment Promoter.

"Oh my God, I know—" I say. But then my heart skips a beat.

Then another beat, then another…

Because the shot on the TV cuts away and shows the viewers at home where they are. They're at a monster truck rally. The camera zooms in on one truck in particular. I gasp.

"It's a pretty genius move," the reporter says. "A real life Bigfoot driving Bigfoot," the man says and laughs.

"*Please*," Athena 'Tina' 'The Killer' Lily Diller says, "the preferred term is Sasquatch," she says comically, horsey, evil. I see the evil in her hippie-dippy eyes. The TV adds 50 pounds of evil.

And then the camera shows the shot and my heart shrinks to nothing in my chest…

It's Starla.

My Starla.

She's inside the monster truck Bigfoot, driving around, jumping over school buses, smashing cars into the dirt. It's obvious she's drugged up or something. The seatbelt is made of chains, trapping her inside. She's hooting, howling, in pain. Her head lolls around on her shoulders. She is scared and alone.

"NO! NO! NO!" I scream.

It's my wail that finally snaps the members of Nine Days out of their TV hypnosis. The singer turns around and jumps up when he sees me. "Why, if it isn't Jason Fields!" he says.

"How did this happen?" I cry. "How!?"

"Because you abandoned her when she needed you most."

"I *didn't* though! I just wanted to play music to heal the universe! It was her idea, for crying out loud!" I shout. "Wait, what? How did you know about—I mean…?"

"You know that stunt you pulled out there, getting them to stop playing shitty computer music? It's not going to work. You're not going to save this worthless planet."

"How—?"

"It's only a matter of time now, Jay, my *old pal*," the singer says and pulls at his face. It is a mask. His face slides off in one grisly motion.

The rest of the band do the same. What is this horror? Before I can understand what is happening, I see that two of them are actually women.

I back up toward the door.

"Hold it!" the singer commands, and levels a Taser at me.

And then I realize who it is.

I shake my head in disbelief.

"Good God, Luke…?" I say. And not just Luke, but the whole Lemaire family. The two sisters point their silver rifles at me. I'm trapped. There's nowhere to run. Nowhere to hide. The Lemaires have me right where they want me. "*You're* the singer of Nine Days?" I whisper. "Wild…"

Luke's ugly sneer is the last thing I see as the Taser's teeth bite into my chest and I crumple to the floor.

The End

ABOUT THE AUTHOR

Well, let me tell you about good ol' Lacey Noonan. Lacey lives on the east coast with her family. When not sailing, sampling fine whiskeys or making veggie tacos, she loves to read and write steamy, strange, silly, psychological and sexy stories. During daylight hours she is a web designer and developer, but mostly a mom.

For more information on Lacey Noonan, why not point your browser snake at:

Amazon Author Profile
amazon.com/author/laceynoonan

Mailing List
http://eepurl.com/bEeNgv

Facebook
facebook.com/laceynoonan123

Twitter
twitter.com/laceynoonan

Email
laceynoonan123@gmail.com

Other Books by *Lacey Noonan*

Seduced by the Dad Bod: Book One in the Chill Dad Summer Heat Series

Amanda's back from college for the summer, sexy and bored. Mr. Baldwin is a chill dad who loves swimming, singing '90s hits, Super Soakers and has a body like a big sack of wet sugar. What happens when these two star-crossed lovers cross paths? And oh yeah—he's her boyfriend's dad? Uh-oh! By turns devastatingly erotic and incisive, this first installment of Lacey Noonan's hot new summery Dad Bod saga will leave you questioning everything in your life.

Hot Boxed: How I Found Love on Amazon

Hot Boxed is the story of Randi, a 20-something girl working at an Amazon Distribution Center who wants more out of life. Assuming she'll work there forever, a name pops up on her scanner that ignites her passions. Does she have the courage to break the chains that bind her, to step out of her dreary life and do something so, so, so crazy to get what she wants? Find out in this super-steamy story!

I Don't Care if my Best Friend's Mom is a Sasquatch, She's Hot and I'm Taking a Shower With Her... Because It's the New Millennium (Book 1)

Life for Jason is one wild experience after another. But then one night, a chance encounter dredges up a long-forgotten mystery, and suddenly he is trapped on a roller coaster of wildness. Is it more wildness than he can handle? Now he is on the run with his star-crossed lover. Will they reach a shower in time, or will the natural heat that burns within her consume them both? Literally, the steamiest book you will read all year!

The Babysitter Only Rings Once

This is NOT your typical babysitter story... One night when Sophie realizes she's left something scandalous at the Lindstrom's—the affluent family she has babysat for years now—she goes against all the fibers of her being and decides to get it back—no matter what, even if it means more scandal. Find out what Sophie recovers in this seriously HOT and suspenseful story by Lacey Noonan.

Eat Fresh: Flo, Jan & Wendy and the Five Dollar Footlong

"God damn, marketing events are bitch." And so begins the sexy, wild adventures of our three protagonists, Jan, Flo and Wendy—the three hottest stars of the contemporary TV commercial scene. After a fight with Wendy's agent, the girls take it upstairs to Flo's VIP hotel room, where they soon discover the pleasures of each other's bodies—as well as the very valuable, last remaining Five Dollar Footlong at the event. Caution: Hottt!

A Gronking to Remember: Book One in the Rob Gronkowski Erotica Series

Leigh has a serious problem. And it's driving a "spike" between her and her husband Dan. When she accidentally witnesses the NFL's biggest wrecking ball, Rob Gronkowski of the New England Patriots, do his patented "Gronk Spike," she is suddenly hornier than she's ever been. This causes her to go on a rampage of her own—a rampage of "self-discovery." And soon everyone's lives have changed. Romance! Sports!

A GRONKING TO REMEMBER 2: CHAD GOES DEEP IN THE NEUTRAL ZONE (BOOK TWO IN THE ROB GRONKOWSKI EROTICA SERIES)

The saga continues! When Leigh spurns his advances at a party he throws in her honor, Dan's friend Chad kidnaps her, stealing her away to his personal New England Patriots Shangri-La, a secret Man Cave hundreds of feet below sea level he affectionately calls his "Chadmiral's Quarters." There she learns about a side of Gronk she'd never known, changing her life forever. Secrets will be revealed—Gronktastic secrets. Possibly the greatest sequel ever written. Makes the original look like a certified *piece of shit!*

SHIPWRECKED ON THE ISLAND OF THE SHE-GODS: A SOUTH PACIFIC TRANS SEX ADVENTURE

Shipwrecked on the Island of the She-Gods is a seriously sexually-charged adventure of heart-pounding exotica that doesn't skimp on story or skimpily-clad native girls with "a little something extra." And it's a little something extra that Noah, Julian and Owen will experience over and over in the steamy jungle, along the shores and atop towering mountains until they're begging for mercy. And then begging for more

The Hotness: Five Burning Hot Novellas

PREPARE TO BE TURNED THE HELL ON. Here are five novellas that will titillate and drive you wild, running the gamut of erotic fantasies. If you've ever wanted all of Lacey Noonan's books in one easy, accessible place for one low price, then this is the book for you, sexy-pants. Contains the novellas: *Submitting the Landlord; Hot Boxed: How I Found Love on Amazon; The Babysitter Only Rings Once; I Don't Care if My Best Friend's Mom is a Sasquatch, She's Hot and I'm Taking a Shower With Her (...Because It's the New Millennium);* and *Eat Fresh: Flo, Jan & Wendy and the Five Dollar Footlong.*

Made in the USA
Middletown, DE
28 January 2017